T0316532

THE MISSING SUNSHINE

Johnson Ametorwo

Afram Publications (Ghana) Limited

Published by;
Afram Publications (Ghana) Limited
P.O. Box M18
Accra, Ghana.

Tel:	+233 302 412 561, +233 244 314 103
Kumasi:	+233 322 047 524/5
E-mail:	sales@aframpubghana.com
	publishing@aframpubghana.com
Website:	www.aframpubghana.com

First published: 2019

ISBN: 978-9964-70-590-9

Edited by Agatha Akonor-Mills
Cover design by: Afram Publications (Ghana) Limited

—— 1 ——

He was a bundle of joy, wrapped in a big white towel when he was brought home. He was admired by all the family. For all his comeliness, he had to be handled with absolute care, so delicate and vulnerable was he. He was named Yao, having been born on a Thursday.

Yao was everybody's responsibility. He was taken care of by all the members of his family in the literal sense of the word— he did not belong specifically to any of them in the household. At any point in time one of the women in the house would be feeding him porridge, changing his diapers, bathing him or dressing him up. Anybody in the household doing the laundry would wash Yao's dirty clothes too. He could sleep in anyone's room. They took care of him when he was sick. When they played with him, he was full of joy. He laughed a lot when an uncle swung him in his arms. He enjoyed especially the lullaby sung for him when he was carried, strapped at an aunt's back. He always fell asleep with a smile on his face.

Everybody liked him. He grew to be a fair, plump infant with round cheeks. His black curly hair was thick and sleek.

As he grew he seemed to develop a natural bonding with his young cousin Celine. Ten-year old Celine was in Class Five at the St. Martins Roman Catholic School at Dzelukope. The first thing she did when she returned from school was to look for him and ask, 'How are you, Yao? I missed you. Have you been a good boy?' Yao seemed to understand her; he would nod and raise up his hands to her to be lifted up. He would chuckle and coo happily, and the sight of his toothless gum sent Celine into giggles. Celine would carry him around for a while or sometimes she would strap him to her back with a cloth and sing him a lullaby while rocking him:

'My little baby, Mama is not at home; Dada is not at home. Please don't cry.'

Sometimes when Yao refused to be fed by anyone they would shout, 'Celine, where are you? Come and take your baby and feed him.' Yao would then eat his food happily.

Even when Celine was doing her homework Yao would sometimes pinch her or pull her hair or her book. If he tore the pages Celine would frown in annoyance, but she couldn't stay angry with Yao for long. There was joy in the house when Yao started to walk. 'Come and see, Yao is walking,' they jubilated. Such was the strong love around

2

Yao who grew into a fine boy.

He belonged to all of them and was not under any one person's constant supervision. He was attended to as and when any person happened to be nearby. Left on his own one early morning, he crawled towards a coal pot on which a pan of water was heating. His inquisitive hands pulled at the pan. His shouts of pain had everybody rushing to him. Luckily the water was not very hot but his infant skin got scalded. They quickly applied Vaseline to the affected part and nursed him till it healed. They told themselves they had to take better care of him.

2

On the main Dzelukope road stood a house built during the colonial times. It was a big house with high walls and roofed with asbestos sheets. It had one big living room, five bedrooms and a porch with waist-high designed cement blocks. It had in the middle of the wall, a concrete frame within which hung a solid wooden gate which opened into the house. On the concrete frame had been inscribed 'Gullit Johannes -1946'. This edifice, known to all as the Johannes house, was the home where Yao grew up.

Johannes was a Dutchman who came to work with the United African Company (UAC), before Gold Coast became Ghana. He fell in love, not only with the country, but also with a beautiful young girl named Sena. He married her and never went back to Holland even after retiring from active service. He chose to settle in Dzelukope, Sena's hometown.

He and Sena had four children— Gustav, Joseph,

Vanessa and Yvonne — who grew up, married and had their own children. Being partly of European stock, the Johanneses were very fair with long noses, large ears, and plenty of dark, curly hair. The natives of Keta called them *Yevuwo*. The Johanneses were a close-knit family. Whether they had a matrilineal or patrilineal relation with Gullit Johannes never mattered. Blood being thicker than water, all that mattered was that they carried the Johannes genes which distinguished them from many other families in Keta. Celine and Yao were cousins who belonged to the fourth generation of Johanneses. Some other cousins were Cyril, Lena, Bertha, David, Anita, Kofi, Joshua and Sena. Some were older than him and others younger. What was never talked about however, was Yao's parents. Yao grew up well, and just as everyone cared for him so did everyone have a right to him. If one said, 'Yao bring me the firewood lying there' Yao would gladly go for the firewood and even push it into the clay stove himself. 'Yao, wash those plates for me,' and Yao would be off to wash the plates.

Yao would pick a broom to sweep at no prodding. At first he had fun, just copying what his aunties and older folk were doing in the Johannes household. Then Yao learnt to bath himself. Once in a while a member of the household would intervene and give him a thorough 'scrubbing'.

Yao was also fun. He could dance and sing. Sometimes

they tied a cloth round his waist and asked him to dance. They would clap their hands and he would dance twisting, wriggling and moving his waist left and right. Joseph had bought him a small drum. He would put the drum between his thighs and hit it hard with a stick. Then he would start singing, imitating songs he heard around the house. The words were not audible but they encouraged him good-naturedly. Often exhausted after the displays, he would drop down on the veranda and sleep soundly. Sometimes they did not disturb his sleep. Other times they lifted him up and carried him to bed in one of the rooms.

When he saw his older cousins going to school, he cried his heart out when they refused to take him. Sometimes they would allow him to accompany them half way to the school or as far as to the school. Then he would be walked back home once some candy was bought for him. One day Yao slipped out of the house carrying a book and a pencil left behind by his cousin Lena. The whole house got alarmed when they noticed his absence. The Johannes family looked everywhere in the house but they could not find him. Finally Amara found him in a shop close to the school. The shopkeeper had seen and taken him in, waiting to take him home when he was free. He had given him his daughter's toy and Yao was comfortably playing with it.

'Ah there you are, Yao. How did you get here? You scared us. Mr. Lucas, where did you see him?' Amara only paused to breathe, confused and relieved at the same time.

Yao only giggled and held up the toy for her to see.

Mr. Lucas said, 'He was walking alone by the side of the road and I realised that he might have sneaked out of the house. He didn't seem to be afraid of the vehicles. I think he wants to go to school.'

A sigh of relief escaped Amara's lips. 'Thank you so much Mr. Lucas. I shudder to think what could have happened to him. He sometimes follows his cousins when they leave for school.'

'Then isn't it time you enrolled him in school?' asked Mr. Lucas. 'How old is he?'

'Four years old. We went to school at six,' Amara replied.

'But things are different today. Let him go to school even if it means only going to sleep,' Mr. Lucas said, laughing.

'And you have given him this toy to play with? Please take it back before he destroys it. No toy remains intact once it is placed in his hands,' said Amara as Yao held the toy firmly.

'Oh don't worry. He can play with it or spoil it. It is for my daughter who no longer plays with it,' said Mr. Lucas.

'You won't believe it. He wants to see the anatomy of

every toy. Sometimes immediately it is given to him he starts dismantling it. A lot of his toys have missing parts.'

Mr. Lucas had a good laugh. 'Oh let him be. He is inquisitive and that is a sign of intelligence. Who knows, we may have a future engineer.'

'Hmmm. Thank you once again Efo Lucas,' said Amara, as she took Yao's hand. 'Let's go home, Yao.'

Amara kept thinking about what Mr. Lucas had said, *an engineer! Even if not an engineer, this young child is showing signs of cleverness and we have to be careful not to lose him like we have lost his mother.*

Amara gave a long sigh and held Yao's hand firmly to cross the street. Everyone was happy that no ill befell little Yao. Now they became more watchful about the little one's movements.

3

Joseph Johannes was married to Amara, a brown-skinned beauty. Their only child, Pauline, was fair skinned with an innocent, beautiful face. While other girls complained that they did not have much hair, she complained about having too much. She found it time-consuming to attend to her curly black hair. She had a broad waist and flat buttocks. She was tall and very slim. She walked briskly, her heels hardly touching the ground.

Pauline was a pleasant personality who got on well with family and friends. She was a neatness freak, who swept or washed as often as she deemed necessary and she was so meticulous about her clothing. At St. Martin's Roman Catholic School all her teachers liked her for her obedience and hard work.

In basic Form Two, she passed the Common Entrance Examination and proceeded to Ho for the five-year secondary education at St. Anne's Secondary School. One day in her second year at St. Anne's she had a mild stomach ache which soon became acute and persisted despite medication from the school infirmary. Even after visiting the Government Hospital the ailment would not go away. Then one afternoon as she lay in bed in her dormitory, she noticed her stomach was heaving uncontrollably as if she was possessed by an inner force. She shook all over and then she fell off her bed. She woke up to find herself on a hospital bed being given a drip. She had repeated hallucinations and began to talk to herself. She remained in the hospital till the end of the term. When she went home the ailment continued to assail her.

Joseph and Amara Johannes girded their loins, they would not allow their daughter's aspirations to be destroyed by this strange ailment. They first took her to the Keta Government Hospital. She recovered for a while and went back to school. But she fell sick again— in broad daylight she was seeing spirits that were harassing her. She would shout and fight them, till exhausted, she would break down and cry. Her parents came for her, trying to console her that all would be well. Sometimes they would hold her tightly so that her fight with the invisible spirits could stop. Sometimes the spirits had the upper hand and she would break loose and take to her heels. Her parents and cousins— all would run after her, grab her and bring her back home. When she spoke she made no sense. Her parents cried quietly out of her view. Other times they just cried helplessly before her, wondering what was happening to their dear daughter.

They took her first to their parish priest for prayers but she was not getting any better. Other priests were invited to also exhibit their healing powers. Once Joseph and Amara heard of any church they were prepared to give it a try: Orthodox churches, Protestant churches and Pentecostal churches. They never ran out of olive oil in their home.

Notwithstanding the advice of relations and friends that they should add traditional healing treatment, Joseph and Amara stood their ground. They loathed herbal medicine mixed with dirty 'voodoo' practices. Some people believed it was plain juju at work, that a spell had been cast on her. Finally they took her to see a juju man in Keta who gave them some herbal concoction. It worked for some time but then the problems returned. They went to a reputed powerful medicine man at Tadjevu outside Keta. They spent almost a month there with Pauline, but she got no better.

Next, they took her to the Psychiatric Hospital in Accra, the capital, where doctors gave full assurance that she would get better. They came back after two weeks. She recovered and her parents were hopeful that the past was behind them. Not long after that though, the ailment came back. They returned to Accra for further treatment. After a month she was well again and she was discharged. This time round, she was well for a long time. But suddenly the ailment came back. Her parents did whatever they could for their daughter. By now their normal life was so disorganised— Amara stopped operating the provision store she had by the house. Or rather the proceeds from the store were gradually used in taking care of Pauline. The shelves in the store became bare.

Joseph Johannes was a pensioner who had virtually spent all his money seeking healing for his daughter. Amara and Joseph did their best for Pauline with a brave face despite the terrible times that they were going through. The larger Johannes family helped as much as they could, contributing money and sometimes accompanying them to places to seek healing. It was one of their own who was afflicted and they showed solidarity and sympathy.

The Johanneses, for the sake of their reputation did not want the outside world to know of Pauline's problem. They kept her indoors as much as possible. When Pauline went out they would quickly go and bring her back home. They kept an eye on her every movement. Sometimes Pauline moved far into town. They would go looking for her and bring her home. There was no need admonishing her, since she did not know what she was doing. Sometimes, she would sneak out before they realised that she was gone. They would look for her in all the nooks and crannies of Keta. Sometimes they would find her in an unkempt state.

They would bring her home, give her a wash and dress her up in fresh clothing. Other times for days on end she would not be seen. Sadly, they had to admit that Pauline was mentally challenged.

She roamed the streets of Keta. They did not know what to do anymore. But that was not to be the end of the woes of Pauline or her parents. To their horror, they found that Pauline was pregnant. Amara cried endlessly. What callous man had done this to Pauline? She refused to come home. They took very good care of her. Amara consulted the midwives at the clinic in town and they gave her the necessary drugs which they put in her food so that the growing child would not be deficient in nutrients. They monitored her movements closely. The kind midwives had estimated when she was due and had been present at her sleeping place, a shed not too far from the clinic. When she started labouring, they were there to deliver her. They cleaned her up and managed to get her to the clinic for a wash. When the baby was taken away from her and given to Amara, Pauline protested and cried but they calmed her down and gave her food and medicine. She slept off. The next day she went back to her shed. Her cousins had gone to clean up the place for her. They were hoping that she would come home because of the baby but she didn't.

That baby was Yao. And that was how Yao became a communal baby in the Johannes household. Amara was quite spent in energy— physically, emotionally and psychologically to undertake the duties of nursing a baby all alone. So the whole Johannes clan got involved to care for Yao.

4

Pauline was left to herself staying out as long as she wanted. That gave her the space to live her life, lost in her own world. Wherever she took shelter, they cleaned the place, provided clean drinking water and change of clothes for her often. They replaced her eating plates and gave her money to buy whatever she wanted. They knew it would be an affront to the Johannes name if they neglected to take care of her.

A time came however, when Pauline could not be found anywhere in Keta. At first they did not feel alarmed, but one whole week passed and Pauline could not be seen. They combed every part of Keta to no avail. The police were informed and despite all their efforts Pauline could not be located. It was presumed that her loitering might have taken her out of Keta to the surrounding villages or even beyond but search teams returned without her.

The disappearance of Pauline happened at about the same time that a boat on the Keta lagoon went missing.

Initially, it was thought that she might have gotten into the boat and been carried away by the lagoon to an unknown destination along the coast. But the boat was located later in another part of Keta, with no sign of Pauline. They thought maybe she had sailed to that part of Keta and continued her journey on foot. The days passed with no sign of Pauline. The family regretted leaving her alone. This mistake would haunt them for many years to come. Sometimes they feared somebody had abducted her. But they hoped that was not the case. They prayed that she would surface in the same manner she had vanished. After a while, she became only a memory lingering in their minds, sometimes faintly and sometimes forcefully.

* * *

Little Yao would grow without knowing his mother. Later on in life, he heard bits and pieces of her story but no one was prepared to tell him the full story. This made him sad. He felt loved but he sensed a persistent emptiness and uncertainty. He did not know who to ask and what to ask. He belonged to everybody and yet felt he didn't belong. He sensed that since nobody was ready to tell him the full story of whatever it was, he will just get on with life and make the best of it. Perhaps, just perhaps one day, he may be able to make sense of it and the void would be filled. Meanwhile, he must show his mettle, achieve something in this world which he could use to console himself.

Days passed into weeks and weeks into months and then years. Yao grew up in a loving family. For his grandparents, he was a daily reminder of Pauline.

When Yao attained the age of six he was sent to school. He had grown into an intelligent, agile and very healthy boy, always running around. One Monday morning in the month of September, when school re-opened, Yao, together with his cousins Kofi, Anita, Grace and Cyril, all of the same age, were taken to St. Martins Roman Catholic Primary School. Yao held the hand of Celine who was now in middle school. The cousins got admission into Class One. Yao and his cousin Kofi looked very much like twins. In order to forestall any problems of twin naughtiness the head teacher put Yao in Class One A and Kofi in Class One B.

Yao liked his new khaki uniform and the matching sandals. He liked the black slate that was given to him. He also liked the neatly folded white handkerchief that was tucked in his pocket. He kept pulling it out and looking at it.

Yao also liked his new environment. The school block was one long building at the end of which was the church building with a big compound. At the back of the church was the residence for the priest and two Catholic sisters—Rebecca and Evangelista.

There was a gated orchard which boasted of coconut, pawpaw, orange, pear and mango trees. A well-kept garden had a variety of flowers which was a riot of colour all year round. In the cool of the night, the beautiful scent of 'The queen of the night' filled the air.

Yao was excited that now he actually entered the primary school building which he had been seeing from a distance when going to church. He would no longer be left behind when his cousins went to school. Yao's whole being bubbled with excitement. Some of his fellow pupils were crying to go back home with their parents. Paying no attention to them, he moved around touching and feeling everything in view. His curiosity was that of a swarm of bees fluttering and sniffing at their honey-laden nest. He moved from one point of the classroom to another, looking at the pictures on the walls. He saw fruits, animals and numbers. He went to his class teacher who was writing in a big book on her desk. She asked his name, he called it and she ticked it. He continued to hang around her. When the teacher was going out, he accompanied her and she held his hands.

'Is this your new child?' Teacher Adjo asked.

'Yes,' his class teacher, Marian chuckled and the other teachers laughed. Teacher Adjo ruffled Yao's curly hair and said, 'What a lovely child! What is his name?'

'He is called Yao Johannes,' Marian replied.

Young Yao showed signs that very first week that he was going to be a fast learner. Once when the teacher had gone out, he went and sat on the teacher's chair in front of the class, picked the teacher's cane and started shouting at the class, 'Keep quiet!' and brought the cane down with a thud on the teacher's table. He had seen the class teacher doing so. When she returned the teacher was very surprised. She gave him a new name, Class Prefect. Soon his colleagues and others started calling him Class P for short or later just CP, a name he carried till he left the school.

Within a short time, Yao was known all over the school, demonstrating immense enthusiasm for whatever he was doing. Some of the senior pupils thought he was a show-off and tried to bully him but Celine was there to protect him.

Yao enjoyed school; he was brilliant and a good sport. Anytime the teacher realised that he did not understand anything, she knew that it was likely his other classmates had more difficulty in understanding the lesson. Yao participated actively in all school activities. He was an all-rounder— he liked physical education, poetry recital and singing. The year passed quickly and Yao moved to class two and then class three. By now he was nine years old.

5

It was a chilly dry morning, the sky was pale blue. The desolate trees with shrivelled branches reflected the dismal atmosphere. It was a few weeks before Christmas and the harmattan had set in after a short rain. On the wings of the dry harmattan wind interesting news floated in, providing new excitement to the Dzelukope township. Godfrey Johannes was returning from town and had passed by the Parish. He was always the first to break any news in the Johannes household.

'I have just seen the new white priest' he said.

'How does he look like?' asked Amara.

'He is a bit elderly.'

The church had been informed a few weeks earlier about a new white missionary priest who had been posted to Dzelukope. The elders had wanted to give him a very big welcome but he had declined any fanfare, not even a small delegation meeting his vehicle at the outskirts of Keta to usher him into Dzelukope. So when he arrived within the week, only a small delegation was at the precincts of the St. Martin's Roman Catholic Church to welcome him.

Father Willems was a stoutly-built man. He had an angular face with a perpetually-furrowed forehead. He had large sharp eyes and thick eyebrows. His large nose was high ridged and pointed. His ears were equally large. He wore a cropped full beard. He looked like somebody in his late fifties. When people got to know he was from Holland they were not surprised as his English pronunciation was not easily understood. Ever since Father Dieudonné, had retired back to his native Belgium some fifteen years ago, the parish had been without a white missionary priest.

Father Nunekpeku had taken charge and after only three years had been replaced by Father Morkporkpor. Now the latter was going to Rome to pursue further studies. He had served the parish for five years. His tenure saw nothing significant happening.

Keta used to be a bustling commercial town, but the persistent sea erosion had made it lose more than half of its size. Most people whose homes had been swallowed by the sea had re-located to other places far away from Keta. Some government offices and some banks were forced to relocate to other regions. Government workers who still remained in Keta were mostly teachers and nurses as their places of work were not affected by the sea erosion.

The parishioners of St. Martins Catholic Church were

happy about the arrival of Father Willems, the Dutchman.

* * *

The church had been built by Bishop Herman. It had two rows of pews and large stained glass windows with different paintings of Jesus Christ on them. On the tall wall behind the altar an imposing crucifix of Jesus rose to the roofing. It had been built to temporarily replace the St. Michael Co-Cathedral at Keta. The parishioners feared that the Cathedral would be washed away by the sea like all the big houses and mansions. The current point of onslaught was the portal of the church which had miraculously remained intact! This was seen as a miracle and attributed to Bishop Herman – a simple but powerful man of God who prayed fervently and spearheaded the growth of the Catholic Church in the whole of the Volta Region of Ghana and whose mortal remains were buried at one side of the church building.

The Johanneses were a God-fearing family. They had a reserved pew in front, not too far from the sanctuary. The fashion sense of the Johannes ladies and gentlemen was legendary and they were very much visible on the social events calendar. Little Yao always made sure he was ready before the church bell tolled and accompany the adults enthusiastically.

Once inside the church however, he would join the

other pupils in the front where he could be his restless self. The children's greatest attraction was Father Willems. Though they did not understand the sermon he preached they found the whole thing entertaining. Indeed, even the adult congregation had a hard time understanding the Dutch-accented English. Thankfully, the Catechist did an appreciably good job of translating it into their mother tongue to enable them get the message.

When Father Willems was not preaching, he sat among the children. After mass, all the children rushed to hold his hands. They loved walking with him around the parish, especially because he showered them with candies.

—— **6** ——

Father Willems was a man on the go. A few months after arriving in Dzelukope he made significant observations. The town did not have any thriving industry to boast of and the majority of the parishioners were poor. The parish hardly generated any money for development. The youth were bored. What could he do to transform the lives of the people? How could he win more souls and build a bigger and better edifice?

When he was not busy he would take a stroll to the beach, dressed in a short-sleeved shirt and khaki shorts. He watched the fishermen's activities, entranced by the way they hauled in their catch of assorted marine produce. He always bought shrimps and squid which Wisdom, the parish cook, cooked just like he enjoyed it back home in Holland. By and by, an idea struck him. What if he could buy and sell seafood to raise money for the things he would want to provide for the parish? That would mean getting a steady supply to a restaurant. The supply would not be a problem but where could such a restaurant be found in these environs? Then he remembered his visit to Lomé, the capital of the Republic of Togo, soon after he arrived in Keta. He had met Father Jean-Pierre Basiru, a parish priest in one of the parishes in Lomé. He had taken him out to a restaurant whose meal he had enjoyed so well. He had particularly liked Mr. François Luckman, the owner of the restaurant who came to have a chat with them.

Father Willems believed that François would be interested in his seafood since he had said he ordered his stock from Portugal. That evening he wrote a letter to Father Jean-Pierre Basiru humbly requesting him to do some scouting for him with respect to supplying Chef François and other restaurants in Lomé with seafood. Soon a reply came that the market prospects were good and what was even more interesting, Father Jean-Pierre Basiru assigned Kodjovi one of his parishioners to liaise with Father Willems and give him all the help he needed.

Father Willems thought about the young men in the congregation. Who could be dependable enough to assist him? He settled on Amuzu. He seemed quite serious and dependable. Following expert advice, they procured wooden crates in which they placed large plastic containers of fish in ice and which were dispatched rapidly to Lomé under the supervision of Amuzu. Additional young parishioners were employed to assist him. The ice blocks they got from the few homes with fridges were not enough. Sometimes they went as far as Denu for the needed ice to keep the produce fresh. A young school teacher, Annie, who ran a small provisions kiosk in front of her house, was one of the people from whom Amuzu bought ice blocks. Seeing how the demand for ice was constant, she took a loan from her brother and went and bought a medium-sized freezer which she used solely to make small bucketfuls of ice for Amuzu.

The fishermen worked harder to increase their catch. Father Willems bargained for and paid fair prices and the fishermen were also happy. He made good money from his seafood business. Father Willems knew he had been sent to work on the souls of men. He also knew that idleness or lack of fulfilling activity could lead men to frustration. Thus, apart from his priestly duties and the seafood business, Father Willems had his eyes on another business. He used some of the money to put up a structure on a vacant plot close to his residence. Father Willems had a film projector shipped to him from Holland. He began to show films on Friday and Saturday evenings under this shelter. A short religious film always preceded the main film which was to be shown. After that, detective films or cowboy films followed: they could be American, British, Chinese or Indian. These were films Father Willems rented from the popular Opera film house in Accra. Initially, the film shows were free. The youth especially flocked in their numbers to watch these films. But later spectators had to pay a token fee. Thus the youth were often seen doing menial jobs to get pocket money. The gate fees they paid were peanuts but over time Father Willems became pleasantly surprised at the amount of money he made from the show business.

It was as if a new wind of life was blowing in the community. He noticed that the congregation at St. Martins Roman Catholic Church was increasing. The religious film showed scenes of everyday Christian living that the people identified with. Gradually this had a positive impact on the people. Soon Father Willems employed masons and started work on expanding the church.

As the locals witnessed these developments, they thought that he had brought plenty of money from Europe. Soon they started visiting him with all kinds of requests: medical bills, school fees etc. Once he was convinced about the sincerity of the request, he was ready to help. Soon people came to realise that he did not bring any money from Holland. The youth who worked closely with him saw how he made the most of his circumstances. Father Willems hoped that the youth would come up with ideas of their own and improve their lot in life.

Gradually the new church took shape. Father Willems

worked hard at it. The large glass windows with motley colours in the church building were overwhelming. New beautifully framed pictures about the important stages in Jesus' life and death on the cross lined the church walls. The new sober atmosphere drew more people to the church.

Most Rev. Dr. Tanyui, Bishop of Ho, was invited to consecrate the church. It was a festive day for the whole town as the church choir led the congregation in singing, drumming and dancing.

Soon after completing the new church, Father Willems turned his attention to a new project— the provision of optical services. People in Dzelukope and the environs had never been able to afford optical services at the hospital. He put up another building next to the entertainment structure. He appealed to benevolent people in Holland who sent him used frames as well as new ones. Next, he selected some enthusiastic young parishioners and trained them to properly run the New Vision Eye Centre.

There had never been anything like that in Dzelukope. Soon the whole of the Volta Region and then Accra and beyond flocked to the New Vision Eye Centre to get glasses because the prices were affordable.

Father Willems took his enterprising spirit beyond the call of duty. The more money he made the more he put it to purposeful use. The school buildings of the parish which had not seen much repairs since they were built in the 1920s, claimed his attention next. The window frames were shaky at the least touch. The doors to the classrooms had been patched so many times over that you could not see the original wood from the new patchwork. He replaced the doors and windows and then began an expansion work on the single storey classroom block. He had the roofs removed and provided strong pillars to support an additional structure on top thus converting it into a two storey block. For spiritual development, he built a magnificent grotto in the middle of the orchard.

---- **7** ----

The Johannes' house not being far from the church, the now twelve-year old Yao was often found with Father Willems. Sometimes he stayed behind after school leaving his cousins to inform his grandparents. The latter felt they should just allow him, given his special circumstances.

Father Willems' well-organised lifestyle saw him having siesta from 2 p.m. to 4 pm., after which he took a stroll through the parish inspecting his projects. Yao normally joined him on these rounds. Communication between them was initially difficult but as Yao picked bits and pieces of English, it improved. Father Willems also showed an interest in Yao. He eagerly ran errands for Father Willems— picking up things, calling workmen and fetching water from the well to water the flowers. Soon, he was taking care of Father Willems' orchard. The reverend grew very fond of Yao and showered him with gifts— story books, shirts, shoes, singlets, chocolate, toffees and corned beef which he took home. The Johannes family marvelled at this relationship between the priest and Yao. Was this God's way of showing he was father to the fatherless?

Meanwhile Grandma Amara was not happy about him neglecting his chores at home.

One day Yao was at the parish when he saw his grandmother approaching with purposeful strides and a determined demeanour. Yao immediately sensed trouble so he rushed and knelt before her, begging for forgiveness.

'You want to be a naughty boy, right?' Amara said and raised the cane she had hidden in her clothes.

'Grandma, I beg you, I won't do it again.'

'So it was deliberate?' Grandma asked and lowered the cane.

'Grandma, I won't do it again I promise.'

His friends who were around pleaded on his behalf.

'Next time, I will report you to Father Willems.'

'Grandma, I beg you, do not report me. I promise I will do my chores before coming to the parish.'

Yao was shaken to the core. He wised up. He made sure he finished his chores before rushing to the parish. Even though for a while his playmates teased him about the incident, Father Willems never got to hear of it. Indeed, a couple of times after church he asked his grandparents whether Yao was a good boy at home too and whether they were not offended by his long stay at the parish. Of

31

course the grandparents did not want to offend Father Willems. They felt his association with Yao was to bring out the best in their grandson— a privilege many a parent in the parish wished their sons had.

Yao made progress in school, he was as curious as he was gregarious. He was always finding time to hang around the school band as they rehearsed every Wednesday afternoon. He was fascinated by the rolling of the baton. Soon he could roll it. He asked them to teach him how to play the trumpet. Initially, they refused. After a while one of them taught him the rudiments. It was only a matter of time that he would be able to join the school band. After the seniors in the last year had completed school, two vacancies occurred. One was given to a boy in class six. The other was reserved for little Yao who was then in class four. Admission to play in the school band was not automatic, though. Approval had to be given by the head teacher who had no hesitation because he was an above-average pupil.

The Johanneses were happy when Yao broke the news to them. One of their own was part of the prestigious school band. Yao, the youngest member of the school band was a delight to watch.

Meanwhile, Celine had completed school and moved to Accra to attend St. Mary's Secondary School. She was maturing beautifully. Yao missed her greatly. Anytime she came back home, everybody would be telling Yao that his mother had come and he felt very proud. He would tell her everything, especially his activities with the school band. Celine would give him a lot of encouragement and a parcel. It normally took Yao a few days to adjust to his normal life after Celine had left.

On the 6th of March, Independence Day, all the schools in the Keta district participated in the parade for school children. The school band played at the parade which was normally held at 'London Park' which unfortunately now the sea had washed away. The parade was now held at the Keta Secondary School football field.

Everybody waited for that moment when the St. Martin's Roman Catholic School band would join in the march past. They watched out for little Yao. Dressed in immaculate, well-ironed pair of white trousers with red stripes at the sides and white shirt he would hand over his trumpet to a colleague and pick up his baton and step ahead of the band. He would roll the baton delightfully from the tip of his fingers, toss it up in the air and pretend that he would let it drop on the ground, kneel down, reverently grasp it and spring up quickly. He would give it a swing, turn it round in a circle over his head with a whirl and then grasp it in the other hand and then pause for a while. Then he would roll it again in a circle over his head with the tip of his hands and bring it under control. It was as if he was speaking to the baton. The spectators would let out a thunderous roar in appreciation. The Johannes family could not be more proud than at this moment. The subsequent speech of the District Chief Executive about the fight for independence did not register with the spectators as much as the display put up by the St. Martin's Roman Catholic School band. They would walk home relishing that sterling performance, particularly little Yao's showmanship.

There was no gainsaying the fact that the Church had become the second home of Yao. He admired the altar boys and was always at their rehearsals on Saturday evenings. When the catechist asked him one day if he wanted to be one of them it was music to Yao's ears. For a long time that was all he had been longing for. He began his training and at the same time attended baptism and catechism classes. Immediately he finished his household chores on Saturdays he would dash to the church premises. Rehearsals of drumming groups and societies for Sunday church performances made the place a bee-hive of activities. Sometimes while waiting for the day's activities at the parish, Yao would join his seniors to play a game of football or table tennis with equipment provided by Father Willems. These joyful activities which engulfed everybody at the parish were healthy and drove away the stupor of the past. The healthy waves created reverberated in Keta and its environs and brought new converts and spectators to the parish.

Sometimes Father Willems joined in a game or danced with a dancing group to the delight of everybody. The church, in all sincerity had changed since the arrival of Father Willems. People moved joyously and with a sense of pride and communal ownership around the parish.

One Sunday Father Willems announced that he was going to the port of Tema to collect a parcel sent to him from Holland. The congregation wondered what that parcel was that was worthy of mention. He came back after three days in a very spectacular and unexpected way— riding a big motor bike! They could not believe that he could ride a motor bike all the way from Accra to Dzelukope. The parishioners walking along the street of Dzelukope that late afternoon were surprised to see their parish priest on that giant bike, zooming past them like a bullet fired from a gun. It was a rare bike in this part of the world— a tricycle that had another compartment for a passenger to the side of the rider. This made it different from the normal two-wheeled motor bikes with a pillion seat. It had a giant engine and powerful aluminium exhaust pipes. It gave a frightening zoom as Father Willems stepped on the clutch. Yao was around to wash the motor bike for Father Willems who supervised the cleaning. And that was how Yao was privileged from time to time to enjoy a kingly ride from Dzelukope to the St. Paul light house at Woe and back. Father Willems enjoyed climbing to the top of the light house and watching the sea, communing with nature. Yao would follow his lead and observe the sprawling sea beyond. Yao found it to be a soothing exercise.

Some elders also enjoyed a ride on the bike with Father Willems to meetings outside the parish or when visiting the sick.

Father Willems lived a very simple life; he had two pairs of strong leather sandals and one pair of black shoes which he rarely wore. He was invariably always in white cassock unless he was working in the orchard or supervising a construction. Other times he wore a t-shirt over a pair of shorts when the weather was hot and humid. He learnt to eat local dishes like *akple, abolo*, and *kenkey* prepared by his cook. He never drank alcohol, his only indulgence being the occasional cigarette. He had stopped the seafood business especially when the youth joined in, their eyes having been opened by Father to grab any opportunity around them. Father Willems was always happy to advise them about life matters and life skills.

He often told them that the greatest joy in life was to bring joy to the life of others and one way of doing this was joining the priesthood. As Yao listened attentively Father Willems' words became the touchstone of his life.

He resolved to apply himself hard at whatever he did. He resolved that he must avoid the distractions of life and remain focused to gain the favour of Father Willems all the time. It was in consideration of all this that the idea of joining the priesthood began to steadily crystallise in Yao's mind. He had heard that priesthood is a calling. He told himself he must wait till the time that he was called to join the people of the cloth. Yes, he would very much love that vocation.

——— 8 ———

Joseph Johannes worked for many years as an accounts officer with the CFAO (Compagnie Française de l'Afrique de l'Ouest). It was a pride to work for such a multi-national company whose offices stretched from France to other African countries and the coast of India dealing in all kinds of merchandise. Joseph Johannes was the manager of all the offices to which he was transferred. He had worked at Koforidua, Ho, Takoradi, and Tarkwa. Accra was his last duty post and he had been happy to finally retire on a good pension which was however not enough to enable him build a house of his own. He had used part of his pension to renovate the Johannes family house, and was intending to set up a petrol service station on a plot of land near his house. After paying for the land, it came under litigation. Much as he endeavoured to have the matter resolved with the family contesting the property the matter could not be resolved. Gradually, he started nibbling at the little savings and pension money left in his bank account when Pauline's predicament had set in and devastated him. He had expected a bright future for his daughter. He never for once imagined that she would end up mentally challenged. There was no doubt that his daughter's ailment had seriously affected him. All throughout their marriage his wife Amara had been very supportive, baking bread to get additional income. But she was becoming weak with age so she stopped baking and opened a provision kiosk in front of the Johannes' family house. With the sickness of Pauline she could not pay much attention to the shop. Those who manned it in her absence could not account properly for the sales and the shop virtually collapsed. Now it was a pale shadow of itself, but the little proceeds enabled them to have the essential necessities of life. Joseph had some treasury bill whose earnings, though small helped.

Though Yao enjoyed the support of his grandparents (who he now considered his parents), he wished that they were in better straits and could do more for him and his other cousins. Some of his school mates rode bicycles to school. Some carried lunch boxes. He wished he also owned a bicycle or had a lunch box. However, he took matters in his stride. He knew that if his grandparents had the resources they would have supported him more. As he thought about it he wondered, did he really have to compare? Many of his school mates were worse off and most of them wished they belonged to his family. He told himself he must be content with his situation. The Johannes family was a respected family. He loved his grandparents for their love and concern for him and the other family members. He prayed daily that God would give them long life and excellent health.

He gave meaning to what Father Willems had been telling them— to grab at opportunities in one's environment. He started organising classes for those in the Johannes household. He was only in Form Two then, but he had the aptitude to help the little Johanneses. He had also realised that he had the passion for imparting knowledge. Children from nearby houses joined in the free classes that he organised. The Johannes household took pride in what he did. They wished his mother had been around to see him. As for his father they had still not had anybody coming forward to claim paternity.

* * *

Yao knew every Johannes family member and their temperaments: his grandparents, uncles, aunties and cousins. He sometimes wondered how his mother would have fitted in. His friends at school talked a lot about their parents. He would come home and ask who his parents were. That question always drew a blank or eyes would turn to look in different directions. No adult wanted to tell him, not even his grandparents. His cousins, without any inhibition wanted him to know the truth. When he asked about his father they told him that they had been told that he had travelled. Travelled to where? That one, they did not know. One day, as they were looking through the Johannes family album, his cousins showed him the picture of his mother. The first time he saw it, he could not take his eyes off the picture. He rubbed his hand over the surface of the picture. Her bright large eyes looked poised for a promising life. She wore a green flowery dress reaching to the middle of her calf. A thin veil of tears welled up in his eyes. Later he took the album to his grandparents who hesitantly confirmed that indeed it was his mother. That night and subsequent nights, he had nightmares upon nightmares. Why should others have a mother and father and he should have none? He would have been told if they were dead. Nobody seemed to have any idea where they were on planet Earth. Realising that he was not going to get any more answers than what he knew now he quickly decided to tuck this missing part of his life into the deep recesses of his mind and get on with his life. But it never went away completely. It kept coming back from time to time and he kept pushing it away. Soon it became a faint, niggling distant curiosity, which he hoped could be solved one day. How, he did not know, but was cautiously hopeful.

He loved to read. From the school library he borrowed books. He also read from his grandfather's library which had the *Children's Bible* that he enjoyed very much. The effect of his voracious reading showed in the English he spoke and wrote. It helped him tremendously in all subjects. He was particularly encouraged by his teachers to sit for the Common Entrance Examination but he was not really keen on it. He was only in Form Two and he had already made up his mind to go to the seminary. He loved the white cassock. He wanted to be a priest, to serve God and his people. Yao's greatest joy was when he was doing some work for the church. He loved his church. He was proud of his church. He appreciated the teachings of his church. He loved Father Willems and the other priests who visited from time to time. On a number of occasions he told Father Willems about his desire to go to the seminary. Father Willems encouraged him as best he could. He admonished him that the priesthood journey was not a bed of roses; it needed self-sacrifice, abnegation and above all God's grace. He had to be focused and apply himself seriously to his books. He told him not to forget that above all character was the foundation on which everything stood. Without it everything collapsed like a pack of cards.

The Johannes family was not worried by Yao's choice for the priesthood. Father Willems advised him that since he was interested in going to a seminary he should apply to St. Augustine's Seminary at Cape Coast which had been established by Catholic priests and monks in 1930. He promised that if he passed the Common Entrance Examination, he would write a letter of recommendation to the Rector for his admission. Sometimes it took the personal recommendation of a parish priests to gain entry. Yao applied himself seriously to his studies, wrote the exams and passed with exceptional grades. True to his word, Father Willems recommended him and Yao gained admission to the seminary. Since coming to Ghana, Father had personally visited the seminary a couple of times and interacted with some of the priests. He was impressed by their devotion to God's work and how they faithfully maintained their vows of chastity, celibacy and obedience to God's call. He had maintained regular contact with the head.

Yao was so elated. Father Willems advised him to continue living an exemplary life, pray continuously and fervently to God because that is the only armour through life's journey. Father Willems also warned him about the temptations and challenges that would come his way but like the Israelites walking through the desert, he must set his eyes on the ultimate goal of becoming a Catholic priest. He also assured him that he would offer him any support that he would need any time he contacted him.

Parishioners of the church also had words of advice for Yao. They assured him that they would pray for him and offer him needed support. They said they would be proud to produce a priest from their parish. His grandparents gave him a last word of encouragement—he was the first Johannes to go to the seminary so he should hold high the name of the family.

Gifts in cash and in kind were offered him as he prepared to leave for school. These gifts were certainly an encouragement and further indication that he had chosen the right vocation and people were prepared to support him all the way. He felt so happy about his calling to do divine work.

9

The intense twilight sun created a shaft of light through the thin curtain over the reading table directly near the window. Yao was on his bed reading his Bible. He heard footsteps stopping behind his window which opened into a narrow path from the main road. Two unfamiliar feminine voices could be heard.

'This is the house.'

'You go and call him.'

'It is better we all go in together.'

'Me I don't want to go in, just go and call him.'

'If you won't go in, then let's go home.'

Who could these girls be? Yao wondered. He continued reading when his cousin Kofi shouted from the doorway that he had some visitors.

'Visitors? Who could they be?'

'Some two ladies from the parish,' Kofi answered.

Yao was getting confused and alarmed at the same time. What could be the matter? He closed his Bible and got down from his bed. He went out to the compound of the house.

There were two ladies who had been offered seats. They both smiled at him. He recognised them as members of the parish but apart from the exchange of greetings and normal pleasantries at the church premises, he had no particular relationship with either of them. He showed the same courtesy to all the ladies in the church.

His 'Good evening ladies,' came out timidly.

'Good evening,' the two ladies responded in unison smiling broadly.

'You are welcome. How may I help you?'

'Oh we were passing by your house and we decided to come and say hello.'

'I see. Sorry, I've forgotten your names.'

'I am Eunice and she is Catherine,' Eunice said.

'Yeah, I now remember. Yes, I think I was in your house one time with Father Willems to say a prayer for a sick person, Catherine, yes I now remember.'

'Yes, that's true. That was last year,' Catherine said.

'And you Eunice, you are secretary to the CYO, right?'

'Yes' Eunice said, still smiling.

'Anything I can do for you ladies?'

'Oh we were just passing by on our way home,' Catherine said.

'Well then, thanks for your visit.'

They got up to go. Catherine held something wrapped in a brown paper. He was accompanying them to the gate when Amara called out, asking about the visitors but making no comment. She then asked Yao to buy her a painkiller from the drug store near the Government Hospital.

The three walked along the road side with the two girls occasionally talking in undertones and giggling to themselves. Yao did not know exactly what they were up to.

When they got to the hospital, Catherine finally said, 'Yao we heard you are going to the seminary, I have this small parcel for you.'

'Oh I have been sufficiently taken care of,' Yao said.

'Please don't reject a lady's gift.'

'What is it?' Yao asked.

'Just a surprise,' Catherine said and handed it to him.

It felt like a book. He said, 'Thank you, that's nice of you,' and they parted company.

The girls kept turning back once in a while to look at him.

Yao brought the medicine to his grandmother and went to his room. When he tore off the wrapper of Catherine's parcel, it revealed a very nice Bible with a brown leather cover. He had never seen such a beautiful Bible before. He wondered where Catherine had got it from. Inside the front cover was written, 'With love from Catherine.'

He looked at his own Bible on the bed. It was a simple soft cover with dog-eared pages.

Surely this must be a confirmation that God was really preparing him for the seminary?

His eyes moved to the seminary brochure on his table. He had lost count of the number of times he had glanced through it. The pictures showed a far bigger school than any school in Dzelukope. There was a large green and white Administration block and a number of dormitories. There were pictures of a small chapel, a clock tower, a well-stocked library and a large dining hall. Then there was a large football field and a basketball court. Some of the seminarians were shown reading in the library. Others were shown praying in the chapel. Yao was always looking at the pictures and imagining himself already there. Life at the seminary promised to be interesting. He prayed, 'Dear God, please see me through the course successfully.' Then he said loudly, 'St. Augustine's Seminary, here I come.'

A day before his departure, his grandfather took him to see the owner and driver of the large green and white Marco Polo bus that plied between Keta and Accra. 'My happiness' was inscribed boldly at the top of the windshield. Efo Kelli was a fair, wiry man in his late fifties with a long thin tribal mark on his left cheek. Grandpa informed him Yao would be travelling on his bus to Accra and Efo should help him find his way to the Kaneshie lorry station where he would get a vehicle to Cape Coast. The next day, Efo Kelli duly drove Yao to Accra and showed him how to get to Kaneshie. He told Yao that on arrival at Cape Coast, he was to pick a taxi which would take him straight to the seminary.

——— **10** ———

The road leading to St. Augustine's Seminary was by the beach. There was the familiar sea and the coconut trees lining the beach which reminded him of Keta. The taxi driver traversed a lagoon to the left and continued. Yao kept his eyes peeled at the road, looking out for the seminary. They passed a hospital and another row of houses and came upon a large football field in front of a block of classrooms. The taxi slowed down, turned off the road and went through an unmanned wooden gate. He headed straight to the tall green and white Administration Block. He quickly alighted, brought out Yao's baggage, took his money and sped off.

Yao let out a long breath as he cast his eyes round. The weather was dull and dry. The whole place was wrapped in awe-inspiring silence. There was nobody in sight. He climbed the short stairs leading to the raised verandah of the large building. He followed the arrow on a notice board to the Administration Office, his baggage in hand.

He reached a room with a large wooden door encased in an equally heavy wooden frame on top of which was written 'Administration Office'. Yao knocked softly and waited for an answer. When a faint response bade him 'come in' he entered to see an elderly white man in a white cassock with a silver cross around his neck.

'Welcome, my son, what can I do for you?'

'Good evening Father, my name is Yao Johannes, I have been admitted to the seminary and I have been asked to report today,' muttered Yao. He gave him his admission letter. The silver-haired man read it quietly. He lifted his eyes to examine the face of the young man and offered him a seat, a hard wooden chair, by the desk.

He picked a phone by his desk, dialled a number and spoke to the person at the other end. 'Hello, this is Bro Gregory, please arrange for somebody to come and pick Augustine Yao Johannes. He has just arrived.'

Bro Gregory gave Yao a reassuring smile which did little to dissipate the nervousness he felt.

'Augustine, you are welcome. I hope you had a nice journey to this place?'

'Yes Sir, I did.'

'I am Brother Gregory. Father Glynn, the Rector of the Seminary, will be meeting all of you fresh seminarians tomorrow. You must be tired. Go to your dormitory, have a wash and rush to the dining hall for your meal. Brother

Theodore will be coming for you.'

'Thank you Father.'

Yao was surprised at being called Augustine. He had practically forgotten his baptismal name since at Dzelukope everybody called him simply Yao.

Brother Gregory handed him a two-page leaflet to fill and return the following day.

Soon Brother Theodore arrived with a stout dark complexioned man in grey tee-shirt over khaki shorts. Brother Gregory introduced Yao.

'Welcome Augustine,' said Brother Theodore with a warm smile.

'Thank you, Father'

'Augustine, meet Jacob. He is our steward at the seminary.'

'Pleased to meet you,' said Yao.

'Okay, let us go now, your colleagues are preparing for dinner. You need to join them. You are in St. George's house.

'Thank you, Father.'

Before Yao could move to pick his baggage, Jacob quickly grasped it.

'Oh let me carry it,' protested Yao. Jacob did respond but only carried the baggage and led the way. Behind the Administration Block was an expanse of well-trimmed field of grass interspersed with well-spaced flowers and trees. The view was breathtaking. From the end of the carpet of grass stretched a big storey building which was St. Theresa's House. It was a typical old colonial building with wide supporting columns and wide steps.

They went past this building to another long two-storey building which was quite modern. Brother Theodore told him that the ground floor was St. Luke's House and the top, St. George's house. As they climbed over the steps leading to St. George's House, two older boys appeared at the entrance. They rushed to relieve Jacob of the load.

Soon another older boy appeared and met them at the last step to the building and said, 'Welcome.'

Brother Theodore said, 'Paul, good evening, this is Augustine. He has been assigned to your dormitory. Please show him his bed and let him get ready for supper. Augustine, do not forget we shall be meeting all the new seminarians tomorrow.'

Two other boys in the dormitory came to greet him, each introducing himself. In the end, he could not remember any name. Everybody had a bed to himself. Beside each well-laid bed was a white locker with drawers as well as a small table and chair. He was told that he could pack his things into the locker. Luckily, his bottle of 'shittor', the savoury pepper sauce prepared by his grandmother was well wrapped in polythene so it did not spill. He removed the provisions and left his clothing in the bag which he pushed into the locker.

The dormitory had large louvre blade windows. The whole room was painted white, was airy and very neat. The back of the dormitory gave a large view of a long garden with trees and a block of flats standing over a hill in the distance.

He was shown the bathroom to the end of the dormitory. Everything looked spick and span. He rushed for a bath and joined the other fresh seminarians to the dining hall. The freshers could be distinguished by the newness of their cassocks.

The dining hall was very long and airy with large windows, bright fluorescent lights and a terrazzo floor. Food in large aluminium bowls sat on rows of tables against which had been placed benches. Aluminium plates and cutlery were on the hard wooden tables that seated eight seminarians apiece. A senior seminarian led in prayer after which one seminarian at each table served the rice and tomato sauce. As food was served, the whole dining hall became animated. Yao enjoyed his food as he took in the cacophony of cutlery noise and conversation of the diners. Prayers of thanks were said at the end of the meal after which all retreated into their respective dormitories. At the dormitories there was hardly any noise.

Yao was happy but tired. Just a little while ago he was at a place called Dzelukope. He was now in a new world.

From his mind's eyes he could see the Johannes family, chatting away happily after supper. He wondered what could be happening back at his parish. The choristers must be rehearsing by now, and Father Willems must be reading quietly or writing at his desk. Yao reached for his Bible, the one with the beautiful embroidery given to him by Catherine.

11

Catherine was in Form Three at Norliveme Basic School. She lived with her parents, Davi Dzidzor and Kofi Nutifafa in the same neighbourhood as Eunice, her bosom friend. Eunice had managed to convince Catherine to become a Catholic when the latter had expressed admiration for the Catholic Youth Organisation (CYO). Over time the two became quite a pair of attention seekers in the church by the way they dressed and carried themselves.

After the visit from Catherine and Eunice to his house, Yao had begun to take particular note of them during the remaining days before he left for the seminary. From the sanctuary where he sat as a mass boy, he realised that they sat on the same pew and often would be talking and giggling as the service went on. Yao had seen the senior usher at least once approaching them and motioning them to be silent. At offertory time Catherine and Eunice came alive as they danced vigorously to the music of the choir. After mass they would be seen weaving through the parishioners looking for their colleagues and exchanging pleasantries. Surprisingly this time they would look for Yao so that they could greet him as soon as he left the company of Father Willems.

'Will you be at the parish this evening?' Catherine would ask.

'Of course.'

'Then we shall also come because of you.'

'Eei, don't say because of me oo! Say because of your faith. Prayer and worship are more of an individual thing than a collective thing,' admonished Yao.

'Eei, Yao, you have started preaching already,' Catherine exclaimed.

'I am just speaking the truth.'

Eunice laughed and slapped Catherine playfully on the shoulder.

Yao looked at the shoes of Catherine and asked, 'Do you girls feel comfortable in your shoes? I am always afraid when I see ladies in high heeled shoes.'

Eunice answered, 'We don't have any problems at all wearing them.'

Catherine added, 'None whatsoever. You know, we want to be à la mode, to be abreast with fashion trends. Nobody should think that just because we're in a small town we don't know how to be fashionable.'

'I see,' said Yao, nodding.

Suddenly a group of young boys rushed towards them. One said, 'Senior Yao, don't let these girls disturb you. Please speak to us one last time before you leave for the seminary.'

'Ahh, you boys don't respect at all,' Eunice protested half-heartedly

'We don't respect? Is it respect to be wearing these high heels shoes to church?' Joe asked.

Peter moved towards Catherine, 'And look at the length of your dress.'

Catherine shouted, 'Hei, Peter leave me alone and mind your own business.'

Eunice said, 'And you, what style of haircut is that? You better remove the mote in your eyes before trying to remove our specks'.

'Stop everybody! You can't be quarrelling before me,' Yao ordered.

'We are only telling them the truth. You remember just recently the President of the Parish advised the ladies about dressing decently to church, but it seems the advice has fallen on deaf ears.'

'Let's go, these boys are annoying me.' Catherine pulled Eunice away.

Left alone, the boys conversed about the basketball training for the late afternoon.

Yao recollected these last minute memories as he held the Bible. He opened it to read. For a long time, his mind could not take in what he was reading. He gave a sigh, closed the Bible and pulled his cloth around him, hoping to be refreshed by sleep. It had been a long day!

—————— **12** ——————

Yao woke up to the tweeting and chirping of birds on the many trees surrounding the seminary. For a moment he was disorientated. He looked around and saw his other colleagues sleeping or reading their Bibles. Ah, he now remembered, he was at the seminary. He also picked his Bible from under his pillow and did some reading. Thereafter, he had his bath and prepared for the day's activities.

The greatest event for the day was the meeting with Father Glynn at the St. Peter's Chapel. The chapel was tall and narrow, not more than seventy feet long. There were big entrances to each side of the church. The high windows had various paintings of Jesus and Mary as well as other Bible scenes. Marble statues of Jesus and Mary carrying the child Jesus were placed close to some of the windows. At the end of the aisle separating the two rows of hard wooden pews stood the raised altar. To the back of the altar was a changing room for the priests. The reverent atmosphere of the church was palpable and one had the feeling of being wrapped in piety. Father Glynn was the last to arrive. Yao was still lost in the sea of flowing white cassocks around him. He almost found it hard to believe his ambition had become a reality.

Brother Frederick, the priest who was the head of programmes said a short prayer. He welcomed all seminarians, especially the new ones, and briefly introduced the other brothers and fathers, who were all tutors. He told the young seminarians what to expect during their seven-year stay. He spoke extensively on religious life, sacrifice or self-abnegation and time management. Giving a little background on the life of St. Augustine, after whom the seminary was named, he said St Augustine was a philosopher, theologian and orator whose extraordinary works and teachings as well as exemplary Christian life, devoid of materialism were the bedrock of the teachings at the seminary.

As Yao left the church that morning he was convinced he had made the best choice— true happiness could be found in doing God's work. They all walked to their respective classrooms, not far away. He saw the huge clock tower at the end of school compound. He mused that it must be the tallest edifice in the seminary and possibly a tangible reminder about the seriousness with which the seminary viewed time.

The time table had the following subjects: Theology, Philosophy, Music, Ghanaian Languages, Psychology, Canon Law, the Old and the New Testaments. The various tutors introduced their subjects and talked about their expectations. This was quite different from St. Martin's Roman Catholic School where they had one teacher for one class who taught all the subjects.

One habit Yao developed immediately was going to the school library. It was stocked with all manner of books— religious and secular, neatly arranged on tall mahogany shelves with framed glass doors. It was next to the administration block. It was the first time he was seeing a big library with a wide range of books. He would develop the habit of going there anytime he was free. Another immediate interest of Yao was music. Apart from blowing the trumpet at Dzelukope, Yao had started learning how to play the organ at church. At the seminary he had more time to perfect his skills. Whenever he felt like doing so he went to the chapel and tried to improve his keyboard skills with the permission of his seniors.

Yao made new friends among his fellow seminarians who were from different parts of Ghana but united by one vocation— the priesthood.

He found his fellow seminarians interesting. There was Gershon, who would not stop drawing. Immediately a tutor finished his lesson, he would rush to the blackboard, pick a piece of chalk and start drawing religious images.

Then there was Barnes. Any time, a tutor was late Barnes would start singing in a soprano voice the songs of a famous singer Yao later got to know as the Italian Pavarotti. Barnes eventually ended up being the leader of the school choir in their final year.

Joshua immediately picked pens left by any of them on their desks. So each day there was a seminarian demanding his lost pen from Joshua. Despite his protestations one only had to go and open his locker which was never locked and retrieve one's pen. It could not be said he was stealing it, but he, just like the others wanted to be noticed in quite a notorious manner.

Decorous behaviour was the cornerstone of religious life at St. Augustine's seminary and everybody was expected to follow the rules. Deviations were not immediately punished. There was a lot of counselling and prayers for any one falling behind. A firm decision to expel was only taken if all these failed.

—— 13 ——

Training at St. Augustine's Seminary was rigorous. The seminarians were made to work with their heads, hearts and hands. The cardinal point was that once they were being prepared for pastoral work outside the walls of the seminary, the training must be thorough and complete in every sense of the word. They were supposed to go out and evangelise and show love, which is more an activity than a feeling; everything about them must reflect the good name of St. Augustine's Seminary. Indeed, the tutors were good. They gave them an excellent understanding of the Bible. They smoothened out doubts and motivated them. He particularly enjoyed the lessons of Brother Michalopoulos. The latter was a short, smallish man, with a visible stoop. He had obtained a doctorate degree in chemistry before deciding to give all his life to Christ. He enjoyed writing and had authored many books.

One tutor known simply as Brother James, inspired Yao with his sense of discipline.

Lateness to his class or failure to do one's homework did not go unpunished. His preferred punishment was asking seminarians to clean the sanctuary so hard that one's face shown like a mirror on the marble floor. If one entered the church and found somebody cleaning the sanctuary then be sure it was a punishment meted out by Brother James. He made sure they appreciated the fact that they were tender souls which needed to be moulded into upright lives hence the correction for the occasional deviations. The students never held it against him.

Then there was Brother Xavier who could match names of all the seminarians to their faces. More strange was how he knew their characters and aptitudes. He invited on a two-week basis, a group of six seminarians to his home for tea during the course of each term. It gave him the opportunity to know the students at close range. It was said that when students were on the border line between failure and success in their examinations, the testimonial given by Brother Xavier tilted the balance one way or the other.

Seminarians replaced their white cassocks with ordinary shirts and shorts on farm days. They shared various farm experiences in their hometowns— from being sent to the chief's for stealing palm wine, to dropping the bucket and running away from a python on the way to the riverside. These farming activities were supervised by two female English teachers Reverend Sisters Christiana and Felicity. The sisters eyes never missed anything— 'Please do not weed so close to one another. You could injure your neighbour,' Sis. Felicity would say. 'Yao, I can see you are exerting too much effort - you lack that gracefulness in weeding,' Rev. Sis Christiana would say. The other seminarians would burst out laughing as the young man from the coast showed his sore hands. He hated weeding but he excelled at the piggery though he had no previous experience. He spent all his spare time caring for the pigs. The pigs grew healthy and increased rapidly and soon the piggery needed expansion. Yao learned to slaughter them skillfully and soon earned the nickname '*muguyaro*'(Hausa for 'wicked child'). But his work pleased Father Glynn.

14

There were two things Yao never failed to do when he was on holidays. He went from room to room to greet all in the Johannes household and they filled him in on the latest developments in town, especially in the parish. Next, Yao would rush to see Father Willems who would thank God for his protective mercies and pray that God would continue to prepare him for his chosen vocation. They would then play catch-up about the latest happenings at the seminary and in the parish. Father Willems always remembered his former Archbishop's saying that, a parish which failed to produce priests for the church was as good as dead. He had done a lot for the parish and was in the process of producing a priest for it. Indeed, Yao's first vacation was a memorable one. He felt challenged to show himself in a different light as a seminarian preparing to be a priest. He realised that the parishioners began to equate him to a priest, a person removed from sin and closer to God. Their comments went from the mundane to the spiritual.

'How nice to see you', 'Eih, you are even spotting a goatee, My child is grown. Please we are praying for you, study hard, on that day of your ordination I would be the happiest person on earth, I will spread my cloth on the ground for you to walk on.'

'Father, I have not brought my marriage to the altar, I am waiting for you to be ordained so that you can come and bless my marriage.' 'Father come and pray over my new car for me.'

Once an old lady said to him, 'Father, have you ever heard the Ewe proverb which says 'the teeth are smiling at you, but the stomach is squealing?'

'Yes but I don't really understand it,' Yao replied.

'It means be wary of people, some are evil— and their smile is insincere.'

'Thank you, Daavi.' He thought deeply about the proverb as he went along.

Initially, during holidays he only assisted in conducting the mass. But in his later years he was given the opportunity by Father Willems to preach to the congregation.

His first holidays saw another encounter with Catherine, who sent Eunice a couple of times that she wanted to see him. He could not fathom Catherine's desperation to see him. At one point he suggested that she should see the priest or the catechist in the church about whatever problem she had. But Eunice always came back that it was he, Yao, that Catherine wanted to see. One evening, soon after rosary recitals, Catherine herself approached him insisting on discussing a matter disturbing her. Yao did not know exactly where they would sit. The office of the priest was not opened this time of the day. He led her to two seats on the corridor of the classrooms, where a small faint bulb failed to brighten the evening darkness.

'Yes, tell me, what is your story?'

'Eih, for all these times that I sent Eunice to you, you refused to see me.'

'If I have offended you, I am sorry.'

'No, I won't accept your apology. But tell me, is that how you are?'

'I am sorry.'

'That is not what I mean. Is that what you people are taught at the seminary, to shun your friends?'

'I said am sorry. Just tell me what the problem is.'

'Do you know Father Leklevi?'

'The one who once worked briefly at this parish?'

'Yes. Where is he now?

'Wheta or something, I am not sure. What about him?'

'Hmm Yao, would you believe, Father Leklevi would come round in his car in the evenings with provisions and money, and ask my parents to let me accompany him to visit the sick.'

Yao said, 'Well isn't that what the Bible says that true religion is to visit the sick...?'

Catherine quickly cut him off, 'What true religion? It was all pretence. Immediately, I went out with him, he would start professing love to me. I don't love him. Once when my father insisted that I accompany him, he took me to a friend's house. The friend was not in but it looked like it was pre-arranged. He had the keys and when we went in he wanted to forcibly have sex with me. I had to struggle with him to free myself. Every time he came I would try to find an excuse but my parents would insist that such an invitation by a priest should be obeyed. My parents have so much respect for him. Why should he be doing that to me? I respect him but I'll insult him before my parents the next time he comes to our house.'

Catherine was getting worked up.

'Take it easy Catherine, how many times has he come to your house?' asked Yao.

'More than five times this year.'

'Hmm! sometimes it is the work of the devil oh. You should find a nice of way of declining the invitation. Maybe if you tell your mother she may find a way of telling your father so that the next time he comes they would not force you to accompany him.'

Catherine brooded over the advice. Finally she said, 'Thank you for the advice, I hope you won't become like

Father Leklevi when you become a priest.' A small smile broke on her face as she said that.

A fat elderly woman, Maaga, approached them in the darkness.

'Who are those sitting in the darkness?' she asked.

'It is me Yao.'

'But I can also see a lady with you.'

'It is Catherine. '

Maaga approached, wobbling through the sand with the support of a walking stick. She said, 'Oh it's you Father, I am sorry, I thought it was somebody else.'

'Catherine is just discussing a problem with me,' Yao responded.

'What is her problem, a young girl like her? Be careful with these girls Father,' Maaga said, turned and walked away.

'These gossips would never stop poking their nose into other people's matter,' Catherine retorted. She got up to go. Yao also stood up.

'Where is Eunice? I did not see her today,' Yao asked her.

'She told me she had a headache.'

'I am sorry for that. I wish her speedy recovery, if you see her.'

Yao walked her close to her home before separating from her. He walked home pondering about his senior whose conduct was being reported to him. Could Catherine be telling the truth? If so, why should sin be dimming the light in Father Leklevi?

Apart from this incident the holidays passed happily.

—————— **15** ——————

Once again Yao was back in school, happy to reunite with his school mates and trade interesting little stories. Yao's preferred subjects were philosophy and theology, which he enjoyed immensely. He believed the two subjects were complementary and led to a better understanding of the Bible. Music was his great passion and Yao had taken the place of the senior pianist who had completed his studies.

Life in today's seminary was not like the ascetic monasteries and abbeys of bygone years where the only thing that mattered was spiritual nourishment and growth. St. Augustine's Seminary had a multipurpose sports field as well as table tennis and poker tables and a large television secured in a locked wooden stand, all stationed at a large empty section to the rear of the big dining hall. Patronage was good among the seminarians except for the ascetics among them who abhorred anything other than the spiritual.

Yao engaged fully in all the sporting activities especially basketball and football, becoming the captain of St. George's football team in his final year.

Life in the seminary was not without its shocks though. Yao remembered that one night he returned from evening worship to find that most of the blankets on their beds had been stolen. They could not believe that thieves could gain easy access to the big seminary but then only three security men could not provide adequate security. Sometimes the seminarians would find that despite all the vigilance plantain, cassava and maize were stolen from the farm by the elusive thieves. But the worst incident that baffled them was the stealing of the chalices used by the priest for the Eucharist in the chapel. How could anybody dare steal the chalice dedicated to serving mass or offering prayers to God?

The seminary reported these stealing incidents to the police more as a matter of routine than anything else. However, four weeks after the blankets theft, the police found some being sold at the Kotokuraba Market in town. The sellers were quickly arrested and they led the police, to the surprise of everybody, to one of the security men at the seminary. When the police wanted to prosecute him, there was another surprise— Father Glynn, the Rector of the seminary, prevailed on the police to allow him to handle it himself. He reasoned that the money made from the sale of the stolen items might have done some good to the thieves, if not to their families. Father Glynn then saw to it that the security man submitted himself for counselling; he was never dismissed. Surprisingly, there was no more stealing incident at the seminary thereafter.

One seminarian, Bernard nearly got the sack. Whenever he took exeat to go home to Takoradi, he stayed in Cape Coast and went preaching to passengers in vehicles plying the town. One elder in a Catholic parish in town suspected that the white cassock-clad lad might be from the seminary. When his investigations proved that he was from St. Augustine's Seminary he reported the matter to the bishop who informed the Rector.

In fact, Bernard had taken the Lord's injunction to sow the seed of the gospel everywhere so why wait to preach to people only when they entered the church building?

The main concern for the seminary however was whether he was collecting money donations from those he was preaching to. Luckily when the administration was satisfied that he was not preaching for mercenary reasons they left him off the hook with a stern warning never to preach again in vehicles or risk banishment from the seminary. Bernard remained a good seminarian and was eventually ordained as a Catholic priest.

Then there was the case of Asamoah whose brothers came visiting one weekend in a beautiful, light blue, two-door sports Ford Escort car. Even though Asamoah didn't know how to drive he convinced his brothers to let him drive. He drove at top speed along the narrow cobbled roads and the next thing anyone heard was a big bang. He had lost control of the car and was heading straight to crash it into the dining hall when by some divine intervention, he ended up crashing it against a wall nearby. He had to be rushed to the nearby Government Hospital for treatment of the bruises sustained. The school authorities took a serious note of this act of indiscipline— to attempt to drive when he had no driving licence. Such a reckless act was an indication that he could be reckless with the lives and souls of people entrusted to his care. He was suspended indefinitely from the seminary!

Yao also had his personal woes. Once when he was out playing the piano, some colleague seminarians came for a visit in his dormitory. One of them, Manso, sat on his bed which provided a view of the garden and the priests' quarters in the distance. When he went back to his dormitory, Manso realised he had inadvertently dropped his wallet. He came back and asked Yao for it. When Yao said he had not seen any wallet on his bed on his return, Manso furiously started attacking him. Other colleagues joined in the attack. Yao was overwhelmed into speechlessness at the vehemence of their accusation and the threat to report him to Brother Gregory, his house master. At the height of the confrontation one of his dorm mates Lartey, came in and asked the reason for the commotion. It was then that Lartey said, 'Leave the poor boy alone.' He pulled out the wallet from his pocket and turning to Manso said, 'Here, I was the last to leave the dorm and when I saw the wallet on Yao's bed I picked it for safe keeping for the owner.' He went on, 'Next time you will do well to investigate a matter before you jump to conclusions. In all the years we've been here has anyone ever complained that Yao has stolen even a pencil before?' Lartey turned away in disgust.

Shame was written on the faces of his accusers. Yao sat down heavily on his bed, simply worn out by the bizarre turn of events. The mood of tranquility and inspiration that had attended his time at the piano was shattered.

From a distance he heard his colleagues trying to apologise. He only murmured 'okay' but his mind was still in turmoil. He could not believe that fellow seminarians would act so rashly before investigating a matter.

Yao forgave them but for a long time he shuddered to think what would have happened if he had not been vindicated. The next day on the way to breakfast, he caught up with Lartey and said, 'I want to thank you very much for yesterday.'

'Oh don't mention it. Incidentally, just that morning I had read in Proverbs that he who judges a matter before hearing it is not wise. Try and forgive them.'

'Oh I have forgiven them, just that I'm still overwhelmed by their behaviour.'

'That's human nature for you. The Bible says, many are the trials of the righteous but God delivers him from them all.'

'Amen.' Yao intoned. Temptation was everywhere, not least, the house of God.

They reached the dining hall and went to their respective tables.

One afternoon Yao received a letter from no less a person than Catherine. He scanned it quickly, wondering whether he should stop reading and tear it up. Curiosity got the better of him.

Dzelukope
08.01.1977

Dearest Yao,

You know it is unusual for a lady to write to a young man and express her sincere feelings. But this is what I want to do by this letter. I have prayed about it and tried very hard to remove it from my mind. But the more I think about it, the more I find myself entrapped in my love for you. Please Yao, you are the missing sunshine in my life. I am seriously in love with no other person than you. I know it is something you may find very difficult to contemplate. But that is it.

I love you. Please just accept my love. Just return my love and I will be the happiest woman in this world. You should imagine how I feel!

This decision to write you finally to spill out my love was not taken hurriedly. I am not cheap. Far from it. You know I have told you about Father Leklevi who used to come to visit my parents almost every evening to request that I accompany him on his pastoral duties. He would present them with provisions and money. It was a pretence at Christian charity. He wanted to sleep with me. I never gave in, not even with his gifts of money and other things. You have not given me anything. But I know in my heart of hearts that you are the only one I love. I know you are aspiring to be a priest. But it doesn't matter. I give you all the assurance that I will keep it secret, very secret.

Yours in love,
Catherine.

He was shocked beyond belief. He wondered what could be happening to that young lady. He thought the previous incident had put paid to everything. He told himself to be careful because the devil wanted him to give in to fleshly desire. This Catherine was a liar and very dangerous. He must intensify his prayers to ward off this temptation. He tore up the letter and as he dropped the pieces in the dustbin in front of the washroom, he recalled

Brother Michalopoulos' lectures. He had warned that a seminarian preparing for the oath of chastity, celibacy and obedience must never succumb to such temptations. What mattered most was the soul. He wondered what he had done to stoke the so-called love in Catherine. How could he help her remove this love from her heart? He picked up the Bible, read some passages and prayed for her.

That evening at confession, he told his confessant about the letter and what he had done with it. He was asked to say the Rosary—the Hail Mary ten times, then the Act of contrition and Hail Holy Queen— all towards seeking intercession before the Lord so that Catherine would cease to be an instrument of the devil lurking in the dark to clog his aspirations.

16

The seminarians were allowed visitors once in a month. Celine came often and he was grateful that he had a family that cared. She brought along an assortment of home cooked food which he and his colleagues enjoyed. He also gave money to anyone who approached him for assistance or whenever he realised someone needed help.

Yao's only disappointment was that despite Father Willems' promise, he rarely visited. He was too busy and moreover he knew that Yao was in safe hands. However, he compensated for his rare visits by regularly sending him money through the post office.

One visiting day as he went to greet his visitor he was taken aback to see Catherine sitting on a bench and waiting for him and not Celine. He wondered how she knew that it was a visiting day. Should he turn back and leave her there? Why all these temptations? Another side of him told him that he must be patient with her. After all, one highpoint of their training was to have time for every congregant. He sat by her and welcomed her. She was looking beautiful and had a basket with her.

'You never alerted me that you would be visiting?' Yao queried.

'I wanted to surprise you,' she replied.

'That is serious. So when did you set off from Keta?'

'At dawn.'

'I can't believe it.'

'I just want to see you and your seminary.'

'See me? Catherine you are amazing. I just can't believe my eyes and how is Eunice your friend and all my people at Keta. Is everybody fine?'

'And if I had not come would you be asking all these questions? Everybody is fine.'

'Welcome once again.'

'How are your studies?'

'Fine.'

She looked round and said, 'I like your compound, Very beautiful and quiet for a seminary.'

She asked, 'Do you mean that all these young men in khaki shorts and white shirts are also seminarians?'

'Yes, anything wrong?'

'No, I just find it interesting that so many young, virile men want to do the work of God.'

'Yes, it's a great sacrifice but very fulfilling if you care about God's people.'

They lapsed into silence. Yao looked at his wrist watch. It was four o'clock.

He asked her, 'So would you be going back today or you would spend the night somewhere in Cape Coast?'

'Oh I'll go back. I don't know anybody in Cape Coast.'

'You must be a strong lady.'

Yao looked at her, and his gaze rested on her gold anklet. He did not know how to move the conversation from there. The silence was disquieting.

Catherine broke it, 'It appears you don't like my visit.'

'Why do you say so?'

'You look uncomfortable. Aha, I sent you a letter about three weeks ago. Did you receive it?'

'Yes, I was about to come to that. Catherine, you know I am preparing for the priesthood. It is as if you are tempting me, Catherine, you should understand my situation. Even if I say yes, it would not help.'

Catherine stared at him, as if daring him to read her feelings in her face. Yao looked away. He said, 'Any priest who does that is not serious, please don't tempt me to do anything like that. Now Catherine, can I tell you something?'

'You are already talking, go ahead and tell me what you want to say.'

'Now, you told me the story of Father Leklevi, is that not so?'

'Yes, I did.'

'Has it not occurred to you that you are putting me in the same shoes? The circumstances may be different but fundamentally they are the same: sexual relationship of a person in the vocation of God.'

Catherine kept quiet for a while. Then she spoke, 'Yao, you don't understand. You don't understand love...' Suddenly, a gust of wind blew up dust and leaves. The sun was suddenly covered by scurrying clouds. The wind blew stronger.

'It looks like it's going to rain,' Catherine said.

'Yes, as for this place the rain is sometimes unpredictable. You need to go now before you are beaten by the rain. I can get you an umbrella.'

Yao got up and made a dash to his dormitory to get her an umbrella.

'Please take the basket of provisions along with you.'

Yao stopped in his tracks and took the basket of provisions

'Thank you so much, God bless you.'

Yao took to his heels. Soon he was back, panting and handing over to her the umbrella and the empty basket.

'If I take your umbrella won't that disturb you?'

'Don't worry, I will manage. Some colleagues have two;

they'll give me one of theirs.'

The rain-laden wind was now blowing intensely. Everyone started moving. Now the rain set in. The wind was so strong that the umbrella kept twisting in different directions and was useless at sheltering them from the rain. Visitors who had come in their cars had no difficulty moving away. Yao and Catherine waited on the veranda for the rain to subside.

It was at this moment that Father Gregory came out. He was surprised to see them.

'Oh, it is Yao. Is she your sister?' he asked.

'She is a friend from my parish in the village'

'All the way from the village? Then she must be a dear friend.'

A gust of wind blew across the corridor causing Bro. Gregory to hold his white gown firmly to his thighs.

'It's unfortunate she's been beaten by the rain. Lady, thanks for your visit and get home safely,' he said and turned towards his office.

'Thank you Father,' Catherine said.

After the rain subsided a bit Yao walked her to the road side where she got a taxi. He hurried back to his dormitory, a little wet but happy that he had got rid of her.

The whole of that week, Yao made sure he made more confessions. He repeated the approaches Catherine was making to Bro. Michalopolous. He felt some balmy relief after doing that. Days would pass before he would get over this troubling visit.

——— 17 ———

Yao always looked forward to the holidays at Keta. As he progressed in school, his responsibilities in the home church increased. In his final year he was given the opportunity by Father Willems to preach to the congregation. Yao always believed that a good priest must have thorough grounding in the teachings of great philosophers and he invested his time in going to the library very often to read the works of philosophers like Plato, Socrates and John Locke, among others once reference was made to their works in the classroom.

Subconsciously, the extensive reading reflected in his sermons. And so insightful were his sermons that the congregation was always happy to see him mount the altar to preach. The icing on the cake was when he interspersed his preaching with appropriate hymns covering the themes of his sermon. His voice was a welcome change; Father Willems' English was still heavily accented.

He also gave talks on various social issues to the various

societies in the Church. Some of these church societies had adopted him as their son and had been providing him some support in the seminary. Everybody competed for Yao's attention— altar boys enjoyed his company, men sought advice about domestic, social and marital problems even though he was only a seminarian who had never even had a girlfriend. He tried his best to provide answers from the Bible and books he had read or what he was being taught.

Soon seven years was about to end. He was on his last school vacation before his very final examination and God willing he would head for the priesthood. He went to see Father Willems, whom he spied in oversized blue jeans and a faded grey T-shirt replacing a faulty part of his tri-cycle. On seeing Yao, he picked a duster and cleaned his hands, exclaiming, 'How nice to see you.'

'Thank you, Father.'

'And it seems school is good for you. You have grown taller and put on weight.'

'Thank you Father. What is wrong with your bike?'

'It needs a little bit of servicing and that is what I am doing.'

'I know you are a jack of all trades, so I am not surprised.'

'Well you see, the engine of any machine can fail you anytime if it is not maintained. It is like the human body. It is must be constantly repaired by prayers.'

'Father you never fail to remind me of the need to be prayerful since I chose my vocation.'

Father washed his heavy coarse hands in a bowl of soapy water, wiped them with a hand towel and said, 'That is it, my son. Well, I have finished here. Let's go to my room.'

Yao followed him quietly as he climbed the old stairs to his living room at the end of a long narrow corridor. The living room's only furnishing were four plastic chairs, a writing desk and a table on which stood a small statue of Jesus over whose neck had been placed a green rosary. For Father Willems, there was beauty in simplicity. For the first time ever, he invited Yao to join him in his bedroom. Yao was surprised.

Was Father Willems sick? Just before the door was a shoe rack on which were two pairs of sandals and a pair of black shoes. Father Willems sat at the edge of his bed and picked up a Bible. He motioned to Yao to sit on the only chair by a small desk in the bed room. Yao surveyed the bedroom again. The small canopy bed had a thick mattress covered with white linen and a mosquito net on the wooden canopy. There was an open wardrobe in one corner of the bedroom in which hung three cassocks and folded underwear at the bottom. On the wall hung a large calendar with the picture of Jesus. From the Spartan nature of the bedroom Yao could see Father Willems practise the abnegation he always preached.

After prayer and enquiry about his performance at school Father asked Yao if he had heard about the impending ceremony to honour him by the church and chiefs of the Dzelukope.

'Yes, that was the first thing I was told by my grandparents. I am happy for you,' said Yao.

Father Willems smiled faintly. 'Well, the church has decided to honour me and the village chiefs have associated themselves with it. The District Chief Executive, I am told would also be around. Initially I wanted to reject the honour. But thinking about it, I told myself it would be one singular occasion during which I can speak to the township about certain things I cherish and which I have always told the church and you as an individual.

'Since I came to Dzelukope God has enabled me to do so much.' He paused and said, 'Pick up that leather-bound book on the table and open it. You see the names of those I have sponsored and I'm still sponsoring from basic to tertiary schools across the country. I also have a list of those whose medical bills I have been paying and those to whom I give stipends for upkeep because they are either unemployed, needy or pensioners. I am saying all this in all modesty. I do not want to take any credit for these. The money for these projects is the people's own money. I took it from them and I am giving it back to them in the form of projects and provision for some of their immediate needs.

'Yao, why am I telling you all this?' Father Willems continued. 'Simply that there are ample opportunities around for us to take advantage of. But we are not able to grasp them readily. Spiritual development must go hand in hand with providing the basic nourishment for the body— not extravagance and luxuries which can hurt the spirit in you. You will soon become a priest. I command you not to concentrate only on the spiritual needs of your congregation, but attend to their physical needs as well. Pay attention to the most needy. Look at what would provide the greatest satisfaction for most of them. I have always been guided by the principle that, working among the Christian community involves dealing with two types of poor people: the simply poor and the poor in spirit. To the simply poor, we provide material as well as spiritual well-being. To the poor in spirit who may be materially well off, we give them spiritual nourishment. Let me advise you that as a priest take excellent care of your body. Do not soil your body by going after the things of the flesh. Always make your body a clean and habitable temple of our Lord Jesus Christ. Jesus loves simplicity and led a simple life while on earth. Simplicity promotes the sanity of mind, the purity of thought and brings one closer to godliness. I exhort you to do same.'

These words of advice struck Yao like a final test to find out if he was really cut out for God's work. He did not interrupt Father Willems. He let the message fill his heart: God himself knew that he was ready for Him. At last he said, 'Father, you have been my father and not just a mentor. Where I have now reached in life has largely been due to you. I assure you that I will always go by your words and I will not disappoint you, God willing. I am happy the church and the chiefs have decided to honour you. You deserve it. May God continue to give you excellent health, and continue to be a blessing to St. Martins Church and its community.'

Father Willems sighed and said, 'Now is also the right time to tell you I am being recalled home. Please keep this to yourself. I shall announce it to the congregation at the appropriate time.'

'Oh, Father you don't mean it. Are you saying you would not be around for my ordination?'

'Well, I can't say at this point. If it is the wish of the Lord, then let it be, but it does not mean I shall not be with you in spirit if that should happen. Mind you, even if I am in Holland, I shall always keep in touch.' replied Father Willems.

Tears welled up in Yao's eyes as Father Willems prayed for him. He walked quietly through the Spartan living room and down the stairs. He looked out at the orchard, the many blossoming flowers whose fragrance filled the atmosphere. The parish had really been transformed. His eyes rested on the school block. They were looking very bright from the new painting of blue and white.

—————— **18** ——————

The Sunday morning weather was very fair. It was as if the clouds had instructed the sun to delay its appearance and just hover in the background until the ceremony to honour Father Willems was over. For the first time in the annals of St. Martins Roman Catholic Church, service was being conducted on the compound of the church. Palm frond sheds had been erected with a special podium. Names on white cards had been fixed to reserved sheds. Ushers helped with the seating arrangements. The chiefs arrived majestically, shielded by large colourful gold-embroidered umbrellas carried by courtiers.

The ceremony began. The more Yao learned about the significance of Eucharistic mass the more he loved it. He had learned that the procession was a pilgrimage of worshippers undertaking their journey of faith to the sanctuary. The choristers in purple gowns edged with yellow led the procession. One mass boy in white cassock followed, swinging the incensor from which rose a grey black smoke heavenward. He was followed by another mass boy holding firmly in the middle, a long cross of Jesus. One hand held the stem of the cross above his head and the other hand held the cross close to his stomach. Next were two mass servers holding lit candles. Following closely were the lectors or lay readers one slightly ahead and holding high above his head, the Book of the Gospels, followed by the priests. Father Willems brought up the rear, flanked by two priests invited for the occasion.

Sisters Rebecca and Evangelista were already seated near the podium resplendent in their white robes and blue veils. After the initial preparation for the Eucharist, Father Dumashie, one of the invited priests gave a short homily about the significance of the Last Supper.

The homily was followed by the presentation of gifts, affording the congregation the opportunity to sing and dance joyfully to pulsating drumming to bring their offerings to God. The offertory procession followed, led by one mass boy holding aloft the crucifix, a long wooden cross on which hung the "body of Christ". Two other mass servers followed holding lit candles waist high. An elderly couple celebrating their fortieth marriage anniversary solemnly followed them, one carrying in a silver tray a chalice of wine and the other, a short silver cup containing communion. Then followed those who were celebrating special anniversaries or wishing to thank God for special favours. They carried assorted items like loaves of bread, crates of eggs, provisions, fresh vegetables in small palm branch baskets, tubers of yams, a stocky white ram and money in envelopes. The Nigerian community in the Dzelukope congregation accompanied one compatriot couple celebrating the birth of their baby. The parents were dressed in beautiful clothes bearing the effigy of Pope Francis. The baby was dressed resplendently in Nigerian national colours of green and white. The procession was closed by two ushers each carrying the wooden offertory box.

When mass was over, announcements were quickly made and prayers said for those celebrating their birthdays. The benediction was said by Father Dumashie. Thus ended the first part of the programme for the day.

Quickly the Chairman of the Parish Pastoral Council, Mr. Yaodzi started the second segment of the function by reading a brief biography of Father Willems. He was born in Utrecht in Holland in 1939. His father unfortunately perished in the Second World War in Poland, and his mother had gone to work in a shoe factory to take care of Father Willems and his older brother, with additional support by neighbours and the church. His educationist brother was now retired and still living in the family house at Utrecht. Father Willems had had an early call to serve God and joined the Franciscan Seminary near

Rotterdam at age sixteen. After ordination in 1956 he served in many parishes in Holland and Belgium. Finally, he came to serve at Dzelukope in Ghana. He catalogued Father Willems' understandably long achievements among which were — the renovation and expansion school projects in Dzelukope; charity to many sons and daughters of Dzelukope; provision of eye-care service and donations to the needy. There was a long applause of appreciation from the people who knew all these.

He called upon Father Willems to step forward and Togbi Afeku IV, a parishioner, on behalf of the chiefs of Dzelukope put a garland of herbs around the neck of Father Willems, the greatest honour that could be bestowed on a citizen by the chiefs. This was followed by a presentation of a stool and the bestowing of the title 'Development Chief' on him. Then the District Chief Executive read a short nicely framed citation extolling Father Willems' exemplary deeds and presented it to him.

Next, the church, represented by an elderly lady of the Parish Pastoral Council and assisted by the two guest priests made a presentation of two pieces of kente cloth to Father Willems. They unwrapped one and clothed Father Willems with it to deafening applause.

Mr. Yaodzi invited Father Willems to speak. Slowly he went for the microphone. He wiped his face with his handkerchief and stood silent. Then among other things he said, "I am humbled. I came to do the work of God in Dzelukope. I expected nothing in return. Our mission is to propagate the Bible. Our key Bible verses are Matthew Chapter 10 verses 6 to 9, where Jesus sent out his disciples to the world to propagate the good news to the lost sheep, win them and bring them to Christ. Our mission is not to enrich ourselves but to give meaning through our work to the lives of others. Simply put, we are to preach with our lives to the communities in which we find ourselves. If we are successful in this regard, the credit does not come to us but to the Almighty God. That was why initially I was hesitant to receive any such honour. When I first came to Dzelukope and started selling fish, most of you wondered what I was up to— a priest selling fish!'

There was an eruption of laughter and clapping by the congregation. When the applause died down, Father Willems continued, 'The uniqueness of being a Catholic priest is being poor and celibate. By being celibate I have all of you as a family to feed with the word of God and equally provide for your physical nourishment. That has been my challenge.

'After the fish business, I moved on to showing films. Then I set up the New Vision Eye Care Centre which provided employment for the parishioners who were trained to man it.

I did all these because I believe it is important that

together we take care of our physical needs as well as our spiritual needs. We must be minded to take good care of the body which houses the spirit. Finally, I want to say that my work here in Dzelukope and its environs is a testimony to the fact that as Christians we must live as one community. We must live for one another. The greatest commandment God ever gave was that we must love our neighbours as ourselves. There is no greater joy than in giving. But we can only give if we lead simple lives. A person who is always chasing after material things would not have anything left to give to others. Please let me remind you that human beings as we are, the body will never be satisfied if it is not disciplined.'

Father Willems ended his speech by announcing that he was being recalled home after serving for about twenty years in the parish. He prayed that others will continue to build well on the foundation that he had laid.

There was a long standing ovation for him. Soon the ceremony was over with the priests filing out first followed by others according to protocol.

Yao was a mass server for the day and noted carefully all that transpired. Father Willems epitomised all that a good priest must stand for and had done extremely well for the Church and the people of Dzelukope. He was sad that Father Willems was going back to Holland. He spent most of his time with Father Willems and helped him pack his things, consisting mainly of the little gifts and souvenirs that he had received from the congregation.

A week before his departure, a new priest was sent to replace him. He was a middle-aged dark complexioned man, tall and well-built with low cropped hair. His name was Father Asante. He was friendly but he could not easily step into Father Willems' big shoes. However, his eloquent sermons in flawless Ewe endeared him to the parishioners. Yao learnt that Rev Father Asante had spent his youthful days at Kpando with an aunt who was married to an Ewe man.

Father Willems took Father Asante through all that he had been doing for the parish and how the profits accruing from the business could be used. Finally he made meticulous arrangements for the future upkeep of those he had been supporting.

—— 19 ——

Yao would never forget the day of Father Willems' departure. The heavily attended morning service was devoted to saying special prayers for him. After the service he put his one piece luggage in the car provided by Father Jean-Pierre Basiru who had come all the way from Lomé to take his friend to Accra. Father Willems obliged all parishioners who wanted to be hugged or have a final hand shake. He put his hands over their heads and prayed for them.

Finally, he entered the car. The women could be seen wiping the tears from their eyes. Children who accompanied their mothers to church that morning clutched at their mothers' legs, asking them to tell Father Willems not to go. Who was going to shower them with gifts, give them a ride on his big motor bike? The car took off slowly over the sandy soil of the parish with everybody waving and some still crying. At the junction to the main road, Father Jean-Pierre stopped to be sure the road was clear. Then he turned right and vanished from view.

Yao's eyes betrayed a sheen of unshed tears. The Chairman of the Parish Pastoral Council, Mr Yaodzi placed a comforting arm around his shoulders. It was a reassuring gesture from someone Yao had always admired from a distance. He had overheard Yaodzi consoling a recent widow lamenting her lack of money to cater for her hospitalised child. She wondered why God would not intervene on her behalf. Yaodzi had told her that the seeming silence of God did not mean He had forsaken her. Then he recounted his own personal tragedy and his faith in God. He was living in Liberia with his wife and three children when the war broke out. They had been abducted and sent to a camp where over 200 hundred people were being held. His two elder children aged twelve and fourteen, were taken away from them, never to be seen again! His wife fell sick and died out of grief and he buried her at the camp. Despite all efforts to locate the children at the end of the war— travelling all over Liberia, newspaper and radio announcements— he had not been able to find them. He had come to terms with the loss and finally returned to Ghana with his only surviving son. He went on to say that despite all the suffering, his faith in the Lord had not wavered. But for the fact that Yao didn't want to be seen eavesdropping, he would have exclaimed in disbelief. Here was Yaodzi stoically bearing his tragic losses and faithfully worshipping God as if no storms of life had ever buffeted him! How would it feel like to be in his shoes? Oh, so even today Jobs existed. From that day Yao's respect for Yaodzi had grown immensely.

Two weeks after Father Willems' departure, Yao went to the parish and found Father Asante talking to a gentleman seated on Father Willems' tricycle. Yao greeted them, his eyes fixed on the tricycle.

'Hello Yao, meet Father Jacques Fontaine, assistant to Father Jean-Pierre Basiru of the Lomé Parish. Oh I'm sorry, I forgot to tell you the bike has been gifted to Father Basiru,' Father Asante said.

Yao's eyes misted over but he managed to say boldly, '*Enchanté.*'

'*Enchanté moi aussi. Tu parles français?*' asked Father Jacques.

'*Un peu,*' replied Yao.

'*C'est un cadeau du* Père *Willems,*' said Father Jacques.

'*C'est ce que Père Asante vient me dire.*'

'*Ici, c'est ton parois?*'

'*Oui.*'

'*Alors, où est-ce que tu as appris le français?*'

'*Au seminaire de St. Augustine à Cape Coast.*'

'Are you people selling me?' Father Asante interrupted them.

Father Jacques Fontaine laughed, 'Father Asante, no

we're not selling you. I like Yao. Next time you are coming to Lomé bring him along.'

'I hear, my good friend. It's getting late. You have a thirty-mile journey before you.'

'God is in control, *ciao.*'

Father Jacques Fontaine turned the key of the tricycle, pressed the pedal twice in quick succession and brought the engine into life. He waited for a while and satisfied about the sound of the engine, zoomed off, shouting, 'Ciao.' Yao and Father Asante waved him goodbye. For Yao that last personal monument in the name of Father Willems was gone and to no other place than Lomé. He had been told that in Lomé motorbikes were the most cherished means of transport. He wished though, that Father Willems had left it to his parish. But as quickly as the thought crossed his mind, he warned himself that he must not harbour such selfish thoughts. Everything went to the glory of God.

Weeks later, Father Willems sent a long letter announcing his safe arrival in Holland and thanking and wishing the parishioners all the best. Father Asante read the letter to the congregation. His letter had distressing news too. He had gone back only to realise that the number of Christians in Holland had decreased dramatically. He said that he was surprised that most churches, including Catholic Church buildings were closed or sold out for other purposes. He said that it was his prayer that the growing and vibrant churches in Africa would come and give back to Europe the spirituality Europe had given them. He also promised that he would remain constantly in touch with them.

Father Asante reminded the congregation that the church has a big challenge on hand. They must all work hard not to destroy whatever Father Willems had built over the years. It would be sad if Father Willems should return to Dzelukope to find his church in ruins and the congregation fewer than he had left it. Therefore all hands must be on deck for the good of the church and God's kingdom.

Since the departure of Father Willems, Yao had felt desolate. Loneliness kept him indoors. He needed time to develop a personal relationship with Father Asante. That was understandable, given that he grew up knowing only Father Willems. Father Asante was nice but he must study him, know him well, his likes and dislikes before opening himself thoroughly to him.

20

Yao walked home nonchalantly, feeling hollow. To avoid being noticed he decided to use the alleys of Dzelukope rather than the main road. A nanny goat followed by its bleating baby upon seeing him, turned and ran away. At another point in the alley a woman in a house shouted, 'Yao, I will not give you any stipend, if you don't go and sell this smoked fish today.' Yao mused about his namesake. He came across a man who had unzipped his trousers but upon seeing him pulled up his zip and walked past him. He turned and looked at him. The man who suspected that he was being watched, also turned and their eyes met. Yao wondered why people would not stop urinating indiscriminately. He walked on. In another house, he could hear a man whistling a song. On the main road, he would have met many more people who knew him who would have engaged him in some form of endless conversations.

He got home, went to look for his grandparents who were surrounded by his other cousins, sat with them for a while and mentioned that Father Willems' motorbike had been taken away to Lomé. The whole family was sad. Yao got up and went straight to his room, dropped on his bed and stared at the white ceiling. He wondered how enterprising his great grandfather must have been to put up such a very strong building which was still in good shape all these years. It was at that moment that he heard some shuffling of feet. The footsteps stopped at his door.

'Agoo' it was a feminine voice.

'Who is there?'

'It's me Catherine.'

Yao got up quickly to meet her. He wondered where in the house he could give her a seat.

'Hi, how are you?'

'Just passing by and wanted to say hello.'

'Would you care for a seat?'

'No, yes.'

'Which is which?' Yao asked, beginning to feel uncomfortable.

One of his cousins passed by making as if he was out of the house.

'Okay, just for a few minutes, I know you are a busy person.'

'Not really, unless I am preparing some topic for a talk.'

'Let me get you a seat,' Yao said and went back into his room. Before he could come out Catherine had joined him in the room.

'Do you have a mirror and a comb? I think my hair is in a bad state.'

Yao looked for the mirror and comb on his desk.

'Can I sit on your bed?'

Before Yao could say a word she sat at the edge of the bed.

Yao gave her the mirror and the comb and looked on as she attended to herself.

'Your room is small oh. Are you here alone or with another cousin?'

'I used to be with another cousin but he is gone to school so I am alone for now.'

'Do you have an album?'

'No.'

'You don't mean it.'

'I have a box of pictures. At the appropriate time I'll get one.'

'Can I have a look at them?'

After a little hesitation he picked up the box on his table and gave it to her. She lifted the cover and tipped all the pictures in the box onto her lap, passing comments as she looked at them one by one.

Yao's embarrassment was rising.

'Do you know that your cousins do not like me?' Catherine asked suddenly.

'Do you know my cousins?'

'Was that not Grace who passed by?'

'I see, you ladies and your little suspicions.'

'I'm going, I have spent quite some time here already.'

She put the pictures back, got up and stepped out. 'See me off to the petrol station.'

Yao accompanied her grudgingly as far as the petrol station and turned back.

When he got back Grace was in his room waiting for him.

'Yao please be careful. You are studying to be a priest. These are temptations. Please avoid them oh. Catherine is a bad girl. She has a taxi driver boyfriend by name Joe who has been driving her around the whole of Dzelukope and Keta. Be careful.'

'Oh Grace. Don't worry. I know how to take care of myself, temptations or no temptations.

'Well, I've warned you.'

Yao dropped down on his bed, lost in his thought for a long while.

21

Seven years had quickly rolled by. Yao and his colleagues had been writing their final exams for one week now. It had been many years of preparations. There were moments of low points with various disappointments. Some of his colleagues had been sent home. There were also moments of high points, when they were happy that they had given themselves to the Lord and this was what had sustained them and given them the energy to press on.

The examinations were not always easy. Some of them had to come back to do a re-write. In some papers, they had scored high marks. Generally in some subjects the lecturers were generous with the marks, others were stingy. One Friday, as they wrote their very last paper the final year seminarians jubilated, hugged one another and sang hymns for joy. They then moved to their respective dormitories where their juniors were waiting for them. There were further hugs and handshakes. Some juniors asked for their seniors' note books or house jerseys. That same evening there was a farewell dinner for the twenty candidates. Present were Father Glynn, Bros. Michalopoulos and Gregory, Sisters Christiana and Felicity as well as other teachers and supporting staff. A long table was laid with all kinds of food. For the first time that evening, each seminarian could eat as much as he wanted of the special food for the occasion. Also for the first time, a sound system played classical Latin music in the background. Towards the end of the function, there was a solo drama performed by Joshua. That had always been part of the end of school farewell activities. It was usually on a religious theme. But this year special permission had been asked to create fun on the night by mimicking the teaching life of Bro. Michalopoulos. After that Barnes came over to sing some moving Italian classical songs. The thank-you speech was delivered by Gershon, the school prefect.

At the end of it came advice from the priest. He told them the path of priesthood was about to begin for them. Some would be sent to poor parishes and others to rich parishes. But whatever be the case they must know that as disciples of Christ they had chosen a difficult vocation. They must win souls and lead the flock. Criticisms would come. They were still young. They must listen to advice especially from the priests under whom they would work.

They must be submissive to the priests in churches they would be sent to. They must not assume that they were the repository of all knowledge and that they knew it all. Humility is the key. Whatever they did they should know that it could be their making or their unmaking. The most important thing would be that all would start with their passing their final exams. The administration expected all the twenty seminarians to pass. That had always been their expectations. But sometimes inexplicable casualties do occur. They must all commit to praying so that they go through successfully. Even if there were failures the unsuccessful candidates should not deem that was the end of their life. Only a few in God's own wisdom ended up being priests. He ended by saying that God had plans for everybody including even those who would not be successful in the exam.

The new candidates listened attentively. They prayed that the cup of suffering would pass them by. At the end of it all, new Bibles and rosaries were shared to all of them. A group photo was taken after which they retreated to their dormitories.

They would leave the following day to their various destinations. Buses were organised to convey those going to Accra and beyond to travel together to Accra before separating. In the same way a group bus was organised to convey those going to Kumasi and beyond travel to

Kumasi together.

The church at home knew that Yao would be finishing school soon. He would be their first priest and the congregation was excited. The Parish Pastoral Council set up a special committee to raise funds for his ordination. Among the activities planned was the production of a special anniversary cloth of the church to mark the occasion. At the end of each month the church took up a second collection for the occasion. The special committee kept reminding them that the ordination meant the church had come of age and an indication of better things to come. They stressed that donating for the ordination of a priest would be looked upon favourably by God. One committee member, Ibe, excited the church with skillful oratory. Tall and wiry but full of energy, he would shout out to the congregation, 'St. Martin's Church!'

'St. Martins Church for Christ,' the congregation would respond.

'I had a dream last night. I heard God speaking to me,' Ibe went on.

'Is that so?'

'Yes, I am not blaspheming, I heard God speaking to me. He said that those who would be contributing to Father Yao's ordination... Did I say Father Yao's ordination? Say

Amen, Yao is already a Reverend Father. God has already sanctioned it. No principality can stand against it. Say amen!'

'Amen!' The congregation erupted into laughter and loud spontaneous applause.

'Yes, anybody who contributes one hundred cedis towards this good cause would walk straight to heaven. Y-e-s...? I see five women and two men to my right. Men are you afraid to accept the challenge? Ushers please take the bowl to them. Okay now fifty cedis, ushers please hurry up with your bowls... forty ... thirty...'

The congregation good naturedly went along with such puffs and contributed very generously. They could foresee that Yao would be a great priest. His sermons made them weep in the recesses of their hearts for being sinners and yearned for God like desert travellers seeking water to quench their thirst. In this case they yearned for God's forgiveness and salvation. Yao was a sociable person in whose company all felt at ease. The congregation was prepared to give their last pesewa towards the ordination of their very own.

The Johannes family had set up a small planning committee to organise a party for Yao and a few invitees. A member of that committee had gone to Lomé to select ladies' shoes, another to Accra to select cloth for the occasion. For the men a top class designer was to sew the latest fashionable coats. An advanced booking had been made at the local Royal Marine Club. The party would be on the evening of the day that Yao would say his first mass. They planned to present him with a valise containing five shirts, two pairs of shoes, a pair of sandals, a set of underwear, three pairs of trousers, two towels and toiletries. All this was in appreciation of the honour that he had done the Johannes family.

Yao had heard snippets about preparations by the church and the family for his ordination even while at the seminary. He was elated and prayed continuously that he would pass his final examination so that he did not become a disappointment to his parishioners and family.

There had been numerous occasions when seminarians with high hopes had not been found suitable for priesthood and accordingly been denied the final call. The process seemed very mysterious and incomprehensible. Some people say that a psychological interview was conducted in the final analysis where the candidates were tested and depending on the answers given they were adjudged qualified or not to become priests. Others still say that the information from the congregation weeks before the final confirmation of seminarians for ordination into priesthood mattered most. It was alleged that once a member of the congregation provided information which was somewhat adjudged to be true on the surface of it, that was enough to disqualify a seminarian. Thus the final weeks before the ordination of seminarians into priests was always a period of trepidation. No matter their brilliance they just could not tell if they would be admitted until the final list of candidates was released. It was only the priests at the seminary and the bishop who understood how the final selection for priesthood was made. Yao prayed fervently to God to go through without any problem. That was the greatest disgrace a seminarian could face—bringing total disgrace to his family and parish.

He always remembered Father Willems and prayed for him. He prayed that all his good mentoring would not be in vain. He couldn't wait to write and send him pictures of his ordination.

—————— **22** ——————

Yao was at home waiting for his ordination. He spent most of his time at the church. People were always happy to see him. The small boy that they used to see around had now grown into a fine young man before their very eyes! He usually began his preaching with a local song or a hymn to psyche up the congregation for the day's sermon. He liked to spice his sermon with everyday life stories and a bit of philosophy, preaching with such ease and grace uncommon for a beginner like him.

Once Yao preached eloquently on the concept of the Trinity. 'As you all know, we always talk about God the Father, God the Son and God the Holy Spirit. That is God manifesting Himself in three persons. This, my dear brothers and sisters, is simply put, how God is referred to as the Trinity.'

At the end of one Sunday service, Father Asante announced that Yao had finished his seven-year seminary course. He was awaiting his results and as was the practice before ordination, if anyone had anything to say against his ordination as a Catholic priest they could see him or give a written report to him. He also called on the congregation for prayers of support for Yao at this crucial moment and that should everything go well, he would communicate to them the exact day of his ordination as soon as the Bishop released the names of the ordinands. At the end of the service most of the parishioners joked happily with Yao. He was happy that seminary was behind him.

*****

Amidst the planning for the ordination came news of Celine's wedding. A few months earlier her suitor, Mr. Nkrumah, and his relatives had come to Keta to perform the customary marriage rites at a very brief ceremony. At the appointed date for the church ceremony, a bus load of the Johannes clan arrived in Accra to find a fully packed St. Peter's Cathedral, the venue for the wedding. It turned out to be the most beautiful day in the life of Yao. The groom worked as the General Manager of Acocla, an American Company in Accra. His friends, work colleagues and alumni from Adisadel College and University of Ghana had turned out in their numbers, so had Celine's friends and colleagues.

Yao took in the elaborate spectacle of Celine's long limousine accompanied by a bevy of young ladies dressed in purple flowing gowns and standing on high pencil heels.

Celine looked exceptionally beautiful that day! He was so happy for her. The whole place was a kaleidoscope of fashionably dressed well-wishers. And the cars! He had not seen so many cars at one spot before— from the groom's party's convoy of four cars to the different brands and colours and sizes of vehicles, the cathedral parking lot could not hold all of them.

As the ceremony went on, Yao visualised himself as an ordained priest standing on a similar altar to bless the marriage of others. Oh that the day for his ordination would come soon!

After the photographs were taken the reception took place at Cathedral Conference Hall where there was enough food and drink for everybody. Yao gave Celine a small card as his present wishing her a happy and blissful marriage. The Johannes party left early back to Keta. Yao and two other cousins were prevailed upon to stay; Celine had made sleeping arrangements for them. The next day after church another reception followed at the Acocla guest house at the Airport residential area. A live band provided music. Good food and champagne flowed. The whole place filled with joyful laughter and merry making. Yao sat through happily. He was surprised with a call to say the closing prayers but he rose to the occasion and said it beautifully. Everybody clapped for him. Mr. and Mrs. Nkrumah promised him that they would attend his ordination.

23

It was twilight. Dark cottony clouds scurried about. Yao was feeling edgy and yet could not tell what the matter was. Negative thoughts wafted through his mind from time to time.

He donned brown khaki shorts and white t-shirt and told his grandfather he was going for a stroll at the beach, about fifteen minutes' walk from his part of the town. He had always loved the sea—that wonderful creation by God which was said to be occupying two thirds of the surface of the world. As he looked at the large expanse of water stretching before him into nothingness he could see a small ship seemingly rooted to one spot far in the distance. There was no fishing activity going on that late afternoon but a few people were sauntering by. Gusty wind was blowing from the sea. He walked on, his feet sinking into the sand and sometimes impeding his progress.

His thoughts were full of possible negative things that could go wrong with the ordination What stories had he not heard! What disappointments had he not seen visited on other aspiring priests? He had known seminarians who had successfully completed their studies only for them to be disqualified. Sometimes no reasons whatsoever were given for their disqualification. He had seen seminarians pack and leave the seminary not so much because they had been sacked but because they had reached a point where upon introspection they had realised that priesthood was not their calling.

Yao knew that this was the most opportune moment the devil chose to hurt an individual, to push that person from grace to grass. He swore that he would not allow the devil to derail his ambition of becoming a priest. He had been faithful and committed to God. He had remained as spotless as could be expected. Indeed, as a Catholic, he believed strongly in confession although, some people felt one could just as well pray directly to God for forgiveness. Any time any evil thought crossed his mind he prayed to God or went for confession. He had made his heart a dwelling place of God. He had shown abundant love to others. He pulled a rosary from his pocket and began to pray. He needed the intervention of Mother Mary on his behalf. For a while now, Yao had been praying and reading his Bible fervently that nothing would thwart his ordination. When he was not at home then he was at the chapel. He knew he was not alone in the supplication to

God. He knew Father Asante, the church and particularly his family, were praying earnestly for God's favour upon him.

At home as they observed his jittery behaviour they advised him to take things easy so that he did not end up falling sick and missing the ordination. The few weeks before his ordination seemed longer than the seven years that he had spent in the seminary. He had dreamt twice about his ordination. They were not good dreams. In the first dream he was being chased out of the church of God by some people. He had woken up shaking, his body soaked in sweat. In the second dream he was being devoured by a lion. Again he woke up trembling and was glad to find that his limbs were still intact. He took comfort in the fact that his dreams hardly came true. When he woke up like this, he did not go back to sleep but picked his Bible and read portions of it.

After walking some distance along the beach, he decided to get closer to the sea. He allowed the cold sea water to caress his feet with a hissing sound, sending cold shivers down his spine. He scooped up wet sand and threw it at the sea. He picked some white shells at the beach and threw them as far as his strength would permit him into the sea. He sat down and leaned against a coconut tree raising his head to follow the flight of the white birds in the sky. For the moment while he was enjoying nature he forgot about his ordination. He watched the passersby—the aged folk trudging over the sand, lovers strolling hand in hand, children playing about happily, and young men hurrying past. There was a chill in the air, and slowly the sea breeze lulled him into sleep. He woke up with a start. The whole place was dark. Every person at the beach was gone. He wondered why nobody woke him up. He dusted off the coarse sea sand sticking on his body and headed home. The full moon was yet to appear. On the sea far away, the ship could still be seen seemingly stationary but this time there was a spot of light in it.

24

'What is this? Won't Yao come home?' Grandpa thought aloud. Yao had not kept so long at the beach before. Should he go to the beach himself to look for him or send someone else?

'Has he heard the news?' Amara asked.

'Who could have told him?'

'Well this world is a small place.'

'Godfrey?'

'Has he gone to the beach to look for him?' Joseph asked, his agitation increasing. What if Yao has thrown himself into the sea? It would be one calamity too many. Tears threatened to fall down his face, but he played the stoic. Then to their relief they heard the squeaky heavy wooden gate opening. That could only be Yao. They all heaved a sigh of relief, bombarding him with questions in rapid succession.

'Why did you keep so long?'

'Did you pass somewhere?'

'Why have you frightened us so?'

'No, strangely I just fell asleep,' Yao answered all the questions at once.

'Where?'

'At the beach.'

'Please next time be careful.'

'Your food is getting cold.'

Yao was wondering, why the special entreaties and attention this evening?

He went for his food and ate slowly. As he ate his cousins gathered around him.

'Won't you leave him to eat his food or you want to share it with him?' Amara called out.

After he had finished eating, his grandfather called him to the sitting room. He found his aunties there wearing mournful faces.

'Yao, Father Asante was here with Rev. Sister Rebecca,' his grandfather began.

'Really, Grandpa, what did they want?' Yao asked quickly.

'They were waiting for you but since you were not coming they left a message for you.'

'What message?' Yao asked in a voice suddenly filled with apprehension.

'Yao, you are a man, you must brace yourself to receive it.'

Suddenly his aunts burst into tears and then he heard muted wailings coming from the doorway where the rest of the household had gathered.

'Just give me the news, what's this crying around me?'

'They said your ordination is being put on hold for further investigations to be conducted into a report they had received about you,' Grandpa said.

'A report about me? I have done nothing wrong, what investigations?'

'That is what they said.'

'Me, me?'

'Please calm down,' Grandpa said.

'Can I go and see them?'

'No, it is already late, why don't you make it early in the morning? We will accompany you.'

'No, no I don't understand. I want to go now.'

'Please listen to us, we will accompany you to see Father tomorrow in the morning. Just take it easy,' an auntie said.

Yao burst out crying, 'I've done nothing wrong, I've done nothing wrong, Okay tomorrow then.'

'I am happy you are confident that you've done nothing wrong, let's allow them to do their investigations. God's wishes cannot be subverted, my boy,' Grandpa consoled him.

Yao got up and went straight to his room. The family followed him to his room. The large picture of Jesus on the wall facing his bed looked pitifully but reassuringly at them.

Indeed, that night was the longest in Yao's life. He was the first to get up and have his bath. The splashing of water in the bathroom was enough to rouse the rest of the family from sleep. As agreed, Yao together with the family went early in the morning to see Father Asante. To their disappointment Father Asante had gone to Accra. Yao was still in shock; he knew in his heart of hearts that he would do well as a priest. He remained in his bed the whole day reading the Bible and listening to the radio. His family came in and out just to observe his mood or what he was doing.

———— **25** ————

Father Asante gave a long homily that Sunday about God and his ways. He said that it was not possible for mankind to comprehend God in all of his actions. Man's intelligence and understanding were limited but everything that God does works for our good in the end. He continued, "As believers our faith should not be shaken by unfortunate events because oftentimes what mankind wants is not what God would sanction." He paused and went on, "When adversity comes, and you are down in spirit, you need three important things—prayer, faith and solidarity with others, just as in the tribulations of Job."

Many in the congregation wondered at Father Asante's circumlocution because that was not the exact message for that Sunday. And Yao was conspicuously missing. Just before dismissing the congregation Father Asante gave one last announcement—Yao Johannes would not be among the soon-to-be-ordained priests. This elicited incredulous ohs and ahs from the congregation for a full three minutes. He told the shocked gathering that, that was all he knew at present and as soon as he got more details he would relay it. He admonished the congregation to pray for Yao and refrain from questioning him since he was emotionally disturbed at the turn of events. Nobody should do anything to hurt his feelings any further. The news hard to believe but the empty Johannes family pew gave credence to the incredible news.

Long after Father Asante brought the service to an end, the congregation sat glued to their seats, some crying openly. Then they broke into small groups and asked one another what could have happened. Who could have gone to destroy Yao to the Catholic hierarchy? They could vouch for him. Yao had led an honest life so far. They had known him since he was a baby. They had seen him grow. Some of the people went to see Father Asante but he had gone straight to his room and locked it, telling his office secretary he was not feeling well. Indeed, Father Asante had not been feeling well since he heard the news. He had great difficulty breaking the news to the congregation. For the short period that he had known Yao, he had seen him as a hardworking and very quick-witted, knowledgeable person, full of energy and ideas. He had the temperament for pastoral work, was focused and knew how to prioritise his activities so that he left nothing undone.

Father Asante had only heard bits of what led to

the refusal to ordain him. He had tried to glean some information but there was nothing convincing to link Yao to any serious misconduct. The Parish Pastoral Council sent a delegation to see the Bishop after Father Asante told them that there was nothing he could do since the decision was from the Bishop in consultation with the seminary. But the Bishop was tight-lipped about the details. He gave them a long winding explanation about the rigorous training for the priesthood. He said that at the end of it all they prayed and asked God to guide them in their decisions. The situation of Yao had been one of the most difficult cases he had had to handle in his priestly life but the church's principles were inflexible no matter the person involved. Yao could not be ordained given the facts at hand. The delegation of the Parish Pastoral Council came back crestfallen. They had no choice but to come to terms with the fact that Yao could never be ordained as a priest.

Celine was said to have collapsed when she heard the news in faraway Accra. She had to be hospitalised for two weeks. Her husband feared she would suffer a miscarriage, but thankfully the doctors took good care of her and she came to no harm. Yao sent her word that she should rest assured that he did not do anything wrong and that they should pray for him and if it be the will of God that he would not be ordained then they should allow it to pass.

—————26—————

From a whisper to an ear it started as a small rumour in a casual conversation — Yao was always seen with girls. Catherine used to visit Yao too often. He was found at odd hours with Catherine; something definitely must be happening between them. After all, how could one be sure that Yao would make a good priest? How could they be sure that he would keep his oath of celibacy? Once started, the rumours gathered steam and took on a life of their own.

The absence of Catherine from the parish did not help matters. Some said that Catherine was pregnant and had run away. Others said her family and the Johanneses had prevailed upon her to leave town so as not to jeopardise the chances of Yao's ordination. Some of the parishioners even swore on the Bible that before she fled, they had seen Catherine a couple of times attending ante-natal clinic at the Keta Government Hospital. The rumour mill had been working overtime and inevitably the rumours found their way to the top Catholic hierarchy, hence the harsh decision. It was only then that those who started the rumour felt some grief at the irreparable harm they had caused.

Yao was surprised to hear such an accusation against him. He wondered whether it was an intentional act by Catherine or some other parishioners. He went looking for her but her parents said that she had travelled out of Keta. He wanted the parents to go and intervene on his behalf that the rumour going round was not true. But the parents were not sure. They must first see their daughter before going to say something which might not be true. They knew that Catherine was somewhat close to Yao. The final nail that was thrust into Yao's coffin of the predicament was when his cousins contacted Eunice to convince Joe the taxi driver to come clean on his relationship with Catherine but he refused. He got very furious and stated that a paternity test must be done to establish the ownership of the pregnancy and that since Yao was flirting with his girlfriend he deserved whatever happened to him.

Yao fasted more and prayed that this cup should pass him by. He wrote to the Bishop and copied Father Asante, protesting his innocence. He received no response. He followed up personally to the Bishop who reluctantly gave him audience but said that given the information at their disposal there was nothing they could do about it. Unless Catherine was seen it would be difficult to reverse their position.

Yao was stunned. His faith in the Church was shaken beyond measure. He could not attend church. His name had been tarnished beyond repair. But he still believed in his God. He fasted and prayed more than ever before. His face was gaunt, his trousers hung loosely around his waist.

The most unpalatable news about him was making the rounds in Dzelukope. Probably he might be sleeping with all their daughters; Yao was a wolf in sheep's clothing. When these rumours came back to him, he cried bitterly at this tribulation. He wished he were dead. All his aspirations had been but a mere mirage, his hope now burnt to ashes and turned into nothingness.

Months passed. His colleagues were now ordained priests. He wondered: how could the world be so unfair, not prepared to ascertain the truth; how could the world be inhabited by evil persons like Catherine; why could Brother Xavier not save him, he who was said to save students in difficult moments?

Meanwhile the news had travelled beyond the small community of Dzelukope. Celine and her husband invited Yao to come and stay with them in the wake of all these vilifications. But Yao politely declined. He did not want to move to Accra. If anything he wanted to move to Adafienu and stay temporarily with Auntie Amega, a distant aunt who was a relation of his grandmother Amara. When he mentioned it to his grandparents they tried to dissuade him; Adafienu had no electricity and no potable water in contrast to Dzelukope. But Yao insisted. He needed to remove himself from this part of the world where his character had been shredded and tossed to the dogs. He needed to be at peace with himself and he believed he would find peace over there. Grandpa gave in. Yao must be allowed to have the freedom and space that would give him healing and solace. He was a young man and this event must not be allowed to create a permanent scar within him. Many in his predicament would have taken to drinking and smoking and ruined their lives in the process. Grandpa allowed him to go.

Early the next morning, before the sun was up, Yao packed his few things and stepped out. He hailed a passing taxi to take him to London Park where he was just in time to board a lorry going to Denu. It was left with only two passengers and as soon as the next passenger entered after him the bus took off. Nobody took any notice of him. He had not sent any advance message to Amega but he knew that she would not turn him away. He had met her a couple of times previously and she had been so nice to him.

27

Amega's house was tucked under the tall shady coconut trees off the main Keta-Denu road. It had a walled sprawling compound. The whole house was a testimony of the wealth amassed by Amega during her stay in Abidjan. She gave Yao a bedroom bigger than any he had ever occupied. Yao was happy with this new environment. It brought immediate solace to his soul. If he was bored he had mango or coconut trees under which to rest. The only noise was from the goat pen housing about seven goats and two sheep. But he was not bothered. This refuge, if it could be so termed, did not end the agitations within Yao. His was a plagued soul. He had sleepless nights. He was going crazy. He was annoyed at the whole world. How could this sort of injustice prevail in this world? Man was evil. Catherine was the devil incarnate.

Auntie Amega however, surprised him by how she bounced about in a carefree manner. She took life with such disconcerting levity, always cracking disarming jokes. 'Yao, food is ready. I need something to whet my appetite. Please go and buy me some *akpeteshie*'. She would drink her akpeteshie in one gulp. She insisted that they ate together. Yao obliged her but refused to join her in drinking. At mealtimes she would regale him with stories which Yao listened to half-heatedly. When she revisited his issue it felt as if she was teasing him but he knew she was serious in her views.

'So you say that it was rumoured that you were sleeping with a girl? But are you not a grown man? And they suspect that the girl is pregnant? Then that is good news. How long is the pregnancy?'

Yao just listened as she prattled on. 'Many people are struggling to get children. Let her give birth quickly. So do you think that if Catherine brings forth and you bring that child to me I can't take care of it? I am not satisfied with the children I have. I believe there are many people like me. We want more children. I want grandchildren to hang around me, to run errands for me. At my age do you think that it is good for me to be going to the kitchen to cook? Don't you think that it is very serious that a handsome young man like you would end up not giving birth to any child for us? That is why I don't understand your church. Why should a priest not marry? What is the purpose of that manhood between your thighs? I tell you, yours is the religion of the white man.'

Yao looked into her face, her temples sporting beads of sweat. She went on, 'Allow the priests to marry as the other churches are doing. This would stop the numerous stories of a priest having slept with this boy or that girl. I am here but I have long ears. So do you think because I don't go to church I will not go to heaven? We are all worshipping the same God, aren't we? I don't think evil of anyone. I don't do evil. I also pray to our God.' She stood up and sat down as if to emphasise her point. 'Mark my words, my son, we shall all go to heaven.'

Yao only listened to her prattle, not knowing what to say in response, cringing time and

again at her prolific use of profane language. 'Yao, everything is good. God always wants it so. It is only human beings like us who do not understand. So do you want to spend all your life wearing women's cassock and going about saying you are a priest? A man must use his organ. It was not created to be declared purposeless. Don't worry. Time is a great healer.'

When they finished eating, Nana, her grandchild collected the plates and did the washing up in the kitchen. Nana was the daughter of Florence, one of her two daughters. The other daughter was Ann-Marie who was still not married. Florence and her husband Fynn, a Fante from Anomabo, lived in Abidjan but wanted their daughter to have the benefit of an English education. That was why Nana was sent to her grandmother at Adafienu.

Amega spread a raffia mat under a coconut tree and was soon fast asleep. She had spent the greater part of her life in Abidjan having been given by her poor parents to an auntie in Abidjan who was engaged in the business of fish smoking. She would go with her in the morning to buy fish, prepare it and then smoke it. Then they would take the smoked fish to Treichville, by means of a taxi boat over the Vridi canal to a market in Abidjan. When Amega was of age she got married and became independent of her auntie. Her marriage unfortunately fell on the rocks. It was out of that marriage that she had two daughters. She soldiered on in life, concentrating on her fish smoking business. She was hard working and managed her resources very well. She had bought land at Adafienu and built this large house. She had left her business in the hands of Florence and Ann-Marie in Abidjan.

Yao looked at the ripe coconuts on top of the coconut tree. He wondered if sleeping under a coconut tree was safe. But ripe coconuts dropping from the top of a coconut tree were rare. He went for his Bible, sat under another coconut tree and read it slowly. He told himself that if it was the will of God that these things should happen then he must accept it, difficult though it was. The important thing was that he knew in his heart that he had never had anything to do with Catherine, let alone impregnate her.

28

At Adafienu, Yao had practically nothing to do. He spent most of the time reading the Bible, praying or saying his rosary. He never went out to any other place. Sometimes when he wanted a change he listened to his Auntie's radio.

Auntie Amega was always shouting at her granddaughter. Eight-year old Nana was in class three. According to Amega, her teachers complained she was not serious at school and did not know anything. Amega was not surprised because most children in the fishing village in Abidjan did not go to school. School was expensive in Abidjan. But Amega was happy to have her granddaughter around and it seemed her constant complaining about her was a way of showing love for her and fearing that if she was not corrected early she might not do well. That notwithstanding, Amega made sure her dresses were washed and well ironed for school. She made sure Nana ate before going to school and gave her pocket money. She fretted over her lateness in returning from school.

Sometimes Nana would not want to go to school, especially when her teacher beat her for getting her school work wrong. As Yao took in Nana's situation, he decided to help his aunt to bring her up in the most appropriate and God-fearing manner. He talked to Nana and took her to school. Sometimes he actually went to fetch her back home. Yao realised that it was because Nana was having difficulty at school that she was not interested in going to school. He decided to help her improve on her performance by teaching her at home. It did not take long before Yao realised that despite her poor performance at school, Nana was a quick learner who grasped her lessons easily. He realised that Nana's situation at school might be a result of the school environment. For one reason or the other she was not attentive in class. He started giving her extra tuition and the little girl soon improved to the surprise of all. Nana happily told her classmates that her uncle Yao had been teaching her. Her friends told their parents and they all came to see Yao to teach their children. Yao did not refuse. He charged nothing. But the parents once in a while would send him some gifts: fresh or smoked fish from the sea or lagoon, some bundles of onions, tomatoes, okro and even money. No gift was refused. Amega was happy for him. The number of children attending his classes grew.'

Initially, she felt that her nephew would go mad over his personal problems, especially when she saw him often lapsing into moments of contemplative silence.

One evening Amega called him, 'Yao, have you taught seriously of going into teaching? I think you are a born teacher. Look at all these children coming to you to be taught. Do you want to establish a school? A school you could run yourself?'

The advice of Father Willems came flooding his mind: one must be resourceful. Even in the darkest of tunnels one could provide an imaginary light to get through it. That was the essence of life but more particularly of any education one received. The seminary education had broadened his mind and sharpened his thinking capabilities. That was an empowering resource he could deploy in his new environment.

'Hmm, may be,' Yao replied reflectively.

'You see that parcel of land not too far from here, where the Hausa man has been growing onions and cabbage? It is for one of your grandfathers. He would want to give it gratis to us so that the link between us and their paternal family would not be lost. If you are ready for it, I'll go and get it released to you. You could start a school there. The beginning is always difficult. You need not start with a full school and a full complement of teachers. You could begin with one classroom. I am ready to help you.'

'Thank you, Auntie, I am ever ready to take the chance.'

True to her word, Aunt Amega acquired the land for Yao. Amega explained to the Hausa man that the place had been acquired for a school and that he should find another farm land. The Hausa man accepted this in good faith and soon got another land for himself.

Amega was known for her parsimony but once she set out to do something, she would ensure that she got it done. Initially, she got some boys to weed the grounds. Then she got some carpenters and masons to come and help Yao put up a three-room structure thatched with raffia to serve as classrooms. And that was the beginning of Good Shepherd School Complex established by Yao with the gratuitous support of Amega.

It was now five years since the start of Good Shepherd School Complex. From a three-room thatched classroom building, the school had grown into a real school of cement buildings thanks to the support of parents and the generosity of a non-governmental organisation which appreciated the good work Yao was doing in the community. The beginning was not easy. Often he had had to weed the school compound all by himself. Later when he could afford it, he hired casual labourers to help him. Getting school furniture was quite a challenge. He had to get carpenters to make the desks for him on credit and he paid gradually. The thatched hut leaked badly when it rained. He had to go and purchase used roofing sheets which were being replaced from a story building in Adafienu.

Paying his teachers at the beginning was a constant headache. Sometimes he had to plead with them to hold on a bit longer; he did not care if he had no money himself. His aim was just to keep the school going. He loved the satisfaction of having a school through which he was bringing transformation to the lives of little ones. Some of the teachers could not keep faith with him but he was not daunted.

Over a period of five years Yao was amazed at the growth of the school. It now had two units of six classroom blocks tastefully built, for kindergarten and primary one to six, an administration block and a hall which served at the same time as dining/assembly hall or entertainment centre. Fronting the classroom was a beautiful garden planted with all kinds of flowers. Beyond the garden was a large football field. The JHS block was under construction and would be ready in a year's time. Not far from the school was a hostel facility Yao had built with a bank loan, for those who wanted their wards to be in the boarding house. Yao had plans for further expansion. He had earlier consulted an architect who had prepared a master plan for the school and which he followed rigorously. Everybody liked the school. It was spacious, airy and located in a quiet environment. A giant sign board just by the main road gave directions to the school. There was another sign board in Denu some five hundred feet from the main road, advertising it.

The school had a population of about five hundred coming from all over Adafienu and particularly from the

Nigerian community in Lomé who wanted their children to have an English education. With time, he had also been able to recruit excellent teachers. And so dedicated were the teachers that the school began to post excellent results, compared to other established government schools around. Some parents withdrew their wards from their previous schools to Good Shepherd.

To top it all, Yao made sure the school had a brass band. Apart from playing for the school they also had engagements in town. He made sure, as had been the case at Dzelukope that it was only the above average students who joined the school band.

The school fees were moderate and the parents could pay any time that they had the money. He never sacked a pupil to go home because the parents could not pay school fees. Some parents and a local non-governmental organisation were generous. They did whatever they could to support the growth of this young school. Yao had bought a fairly used pick up for a song from one parent. This had helped in carting logistics to and from the school. Again, Yao was able to buy another fairly used bus to convey some pupils who lived far from the school. Both the pick-up and the bus sported the name of the school and the logo, an antelope springing through a bush.

Yao did not forget his farming activities in the seminary. He acquired a parcel of land not far from the school. There he planted rows and rows of onions, tomatoes, okro and pepper. To this he added a big piggery and recruited some farm hands to help him.

The returns from the farming he invested in the expansion of the school.

Yao was happy with what he had achieved within five years. It was well beyond his imagination.

He never forgot his God. He prayed fervently. The pain of his rejection from the priesthood was not totally gone, but with time it had reduced.

Once a while, he went to Dzelukope to see the Johannes family. But he went in the evenings, the darkness shielding him from inquisitive eyes. He carried along gifts to his grandparents and the others. They were happy for him. The Johannes family had forgotten the disgrace that his inability to be ordained brought to them. The congregation and the people of Dzelukope after hurling all kinds of unkind and unsavoury words at the family had now left them in peace.

Having worked with the resourceful Father Willems, Yao brought all the lessons learnt to his own enterprises and reaped beautifully. Auntie Amega pestered him about marriage but each time Yao pushed away the idea. A number of girls visited under the pretext of seeing Amega and always engaged him in a chat but he was just not interested in any feminine liaison. What mattered to him for now were his God, school and farming activities.

———— 30 ————

Despite the success there were moments when he remembered what might have been, but Yao never wavered in faith or worshipping God. He encouraged himself that he was not the first to be challenged in life and he would not be the last. He remembered the story of Job in the Bible. At a point Yao told himself that it was not enough to worship at home. He checked out the Catholic Church at Adafienu, not too far from his home. The newly built St. Theodore's Catholic Church was an imposing rotund glass chapel more airy than the St. Martin's Church at Dzelukope.

The first time Yao stepped into the church he felt an inner joy. It was such a beautiful place to worship in. There was nobody in sight. He knelt down and prayed. Then he stood up, and went round the church quietly. In one corner of the church he saw a fair elderly woman sitting and gazing steadily ahead of her. He wondered what she was doing there. It was obvious she was in a world of her own and barely aware of him. He looked long and hard at her. She was graceful and tall. Her narrow furrowed forehead hinted of years of suffering. The small scarf on her head covered only a portion of her silvery black kinky hair. Her eyebrows were very thick and she had a long pointed nose. She wore a long threadbare dress and small earrings. It turned out she was a fixture in the church—at any service morning, afternoon or evening. She was not always the passive person he saw the first time. The remarkable thing about her was her service to the church. Congregation members normally cleaned the chapel and its surroundings every Saturday and she joined in the cleaning. After a little while she took that job as her personal responsibility, cleaning from inside the church through the sacristy to the compound. When she was not sweeping, she was picking pieces of paper or burning rubbish at one end of the church. The congregation liked her and though she accepted the small gifts they showered on her, nobody could engage her in any meaningful conversation. She never accepted paper money, only coins, as if her credo was to live an ascetic life. She had arrived quietly at the parish some ten years earlier, looking haggard and unkempt. When she spoke, and she hardly did, her accent had a trace of the Ewe spoken in Togo showing she might be a Togolese or had sojourned there for a long time. But nobody bothered to trace her roots.

Everybody in the parish called her Mama Lucy, nobody knew how that came to be. The priest provided her with food daily. When some parishioners attempted to drive her away the priest reminded them of Jesus' admonition that, "Whatsoever you do to the least of my brothers, that you do unto me." Thus compassion replaced rejection and the women supplied her with clothing, showed her a place to shower and provided her hygienic needs.

Yao's heart swelled with compassion for her. Curiously, each time he saw her he felt an indescribable feeling of affinity, a feeling he found difficult to fathom. He showered her with all kinds of gifts and the idea of moving her from sleeping in the corner of the church to a better place kept pricking him like a needle. He even contemplated adopting her if possible. At least it could fill the void in him of not having had a mother.

When Yao approached the Chairman of the Parish Pastoral Council with his request he directed him to the parish priest. Father Heartwill assured him that he had no objection if only she would agree to leave the parish compound. But she preferred the comfort of the church premises. She was not the least impressed by the new clothing and toiletries lavished on her by Yao. But Yao patiently persisted over a long period.

Meanwhile there was a noticeable change— the gradual recovery of Lucy. Her speech was becoming a bit audible.

Father Heartwill took note of this miracle.

One day she mentioned her name. It came off in a drawl, P- a-a-u- l-a-a. She was called Paula. Nobody could ascertain the truth. But she was consistent about that name. So she came to have two names, Lucy or Paula. Yao continued to show love to this poor woman.

——— 31 ———

In the course of time Catherine had returned to Dzelukope, she who had played the femme fatale and caused Yao his priesthood. Initially when she had heard of Yao's ordination fiasco she had been indifferent. But with the passing of the years the falsehood she held in her being was poisoning and irritating her peace of mind such that she could no longer handle it.

She had gone to the new Parish President Dzato to confide in him and asked that the message be conveyed to the Parish Priest. They listened to her and tried to do what was necessary even though they took all that she said with a pinch of salt. Soon the news got to Father Asante and the Bishop. But there was little they could do. Over the years they had been made aware that the institution must be seen as infallible and must be protected. Maybe the people who run it may be fallible but not the institution. So once a decision was made they never reversed it.

Yao had been falsely accused, tortured and disgraced

for seven long years. He thanked God that the truth had come out finally. But to what end; too little, too late. Anytime he recalled that his colleagues were priests in parishes all over Ghana and even overseas the pain had been unbearable. He could walk with his head held high anytime he visited Dzelukope. He prayed fervently to God and wrote a long letter to Rev. Father Asante and the Bishop hoping that the records would be set straight at least for posterity and that his name would not carry a negative connotation in the records.

As he reflected on his life he felt satisfied that he had not wasted his life. The door to priesthood had been closed in his face, but another door had been opened for him. Even as an educationist, he was doing God's work, providing education to many children at Adafienu and beyond. Three days a week, he organised Bible lessons for them. And he was happy about the way the little ones responded to his biblical teachings.

He was a very active member of the Men's Fellowship of the St. Theodore Catholic Church and represented them diligently on the Parish Pastoral Council. The new church needed renovation from time to time to maintain its plush look. Yao contributed as much as he could. He donated choir robes and an organ to the church.

Amega accompanied him to church during Easter, Christmas or the funeral service of somebody she knew.

She rejected Yao's entreaties to join Catholic Church, retorting that as a deist, any religion was sufficient and she was happy where she belonged. Amega insisted that Yao should take a wife and Yao insisted Amega should be baptised into the Catholic Church. Apart from this tug of war the two got on very well.

——— 32 ———

Ohne bright day Yao received a pleasant surprise, a letter signed by the Bishop of the Keta-Akatsi diocese informing him that he was among those to be awarded that year. That award went to very few Catholics whose devotion to God was astounding. Was that intended to compensate him for the mistakes of the past by the institution he revered so much?

The Diocesan Award was to be celebrated by Rev. Father Heartwill. On the appointed day the Bishop would be visiting together with the Pro-nuncio and a retinue of priests. It was a special day in the life of St. Theodore Roman Catholic Church, the first ever official visit of the Pro-nuncio. The church was overflowing that day. He felt that what should have happened during his failed ordination would happen this time around.

Yao sat in the front pew with Amega, Nana, his grandparents and a large retinue of the Johannes family from Dzelukope and beyond. A good number of parishioners from St. Martins Roman Catholic Church came in two buses. Celine and her husband and their two children came from Accra. They had missed the ordination but would not miss this occasion to show solidarity to Yao.

Yao was attired in a flowing white *boubou* with a thin gold necklace around his neck. Behind the Johannes family and occupying a third of the pews were the school children from Good Shepherd School. They had come in their numbers to honour the founder and headmaster of their school. The church service led by the Pro-nuncio with Father Asante as co-celebrant was brief. It was followed by the award ceremony. The Pro-nuncio explained the significance of the award— the nominee must have rendered exceptional service to the church; been at the forefront of propagating the good news; must have brought honour and respect to the church; must be an outstanding Catholic, whose life must have touched many in and outside the church.

The Pro-nuncio invited Yao to the front of the sacristy and read out the short glass-framed citation as follows:

Catholic Diocese of Keta-Ho Office of His Highness the Bishop Meritorious award to you

MR. AUGUSTINE YAO JOHANNES

of the St. Theodore Roman Catholic Church, Adafienu, Denu in the Volta Region.

For your dedication to God and immense contribution to the growth of the St. Theodore Roman Catholic Church and the community at large at Adafienu,

His Highness the Bishop of the Keta-Ho Diocese bestows on you this award.'

The citation was accompanied by a pendant. Yao gratefully accepted the award and dedicated it jointly to St. Theodore's and St. Martin's Roman Catholic churches, Father Willems and above all, to the Johannes family.

Celine led the way with the other members of the Johannes family joining her at the altar to hug and kiss Yao. In fact, Celine dropped to her knees at a point to pray and thank God for this moment. It was as if it was a cleansing moment for Yao and the family— being cleansed of the vilifications and insults when the matter of Catherine and the pregnancy came up.

After the service pictures were taken with the Pronuncio and the other priests, with other church members and all his family members.

A grand reception was held at the forecourt of the church. Yao happily moved among the well-wishers showing his appreciation. People were really enjoying themselves.

Amara was returning from the washroom to the reception when her eyes fell upon a lady sitting quietly and gazing with unseeing eyes into the horizon. She looked at her, wondering why with all the conviviality around one should be so isolated. As she turned to go, the object of her study turned to swat at a fly on her arm. In the process Amara caught a glimpse of her profile. Amara stopped short. She felt a jolt to her heart, there was a faint hint of familiarity about the lady. She could not believe her eyes. She stood transfixed, her heart beating wildly. Despite the many years that had passed she could not be mistaken. She must be the one. Amara shouted, rushed and jumped to embrace the lady. Her hysteria found people rushing to her assistance. The lady just sat there looking askance. Everybody was asking what was happening to Amara. Grandpa Joseph and others rushed to the scene. There was Amara jumping and crying that she had found her daughter. The others added their degree of hysteria. Yao came upon the melée and could not believe the drama that was unfolding. They told him that the woman he had come to know as Lucy/Paula was his mother, Yao just stood there, shocked into inaction, a thousand and one emotions chasing one another inside him.

First of all Amara had to be calmed down. Joseph could also not believe what was happening. Indeed, this was their daughter. For the Johannes family the party was over. Yao rushed to bring his mini-bus. Strangely, without protest, Pauline was helped into the vehicle. Together with her belongings and she was driven quietly away to the home of Yao.

The family feasted their eyes on her; they danced in ecstasy. Attempts to elicit any response from her met with mumblings. That did not matter, they were happy to discover their family member. For those who still doubted that this was Pauline, Amara showed them her birthmark, a black spot in the middle of Pauline's lower lip.

The merrymaking extended to the house. Assorted drinks flowed, and the appetizing aroma of chicken and goat soup wafted into the sitting room from the kitchen. Joyous laughter floated in the air. Joseph Johannes sat quietly through all this, overpowered by an inexplicable emotion. He bent his head and started crying. A cousin lifted up his chin and asked, 'Are you not a man? This is the day the Lord has made for us to rejoice.'

'I just don't understand. I just don't understand,' Joseph mumbled. 'Auntie Amega, do you say that you are in this village for all this while and you don't know that your cousin is living so close to you?'

'I'm surprised myself. If I were to attend church, then you could blame me,' Auntie Amega responded.

'You see how important it is to attend church and the blessings you can get from the Lord?' Amara reproached her. Amega had no answer to that. She only called out, 'Agovi, where are you?' When the young boy came running she said, 'Kindly get me a bottle of drink.' He rushed off to go and buy *akpeteshie,* Amega's favourite gin. Right now she needed the drink to swallow her amazement.

Yao sat on a sofa across from his mother. He just sat there looking intently at her and taking in all that was happening around him. Was there never an end to surprises?

Eventually the family prepared to leave. Pauline did not put up any resistance when they took her with them.

——— 33 ———

Weeks after the ceremony, Yao had a surprise visit from Father Asante bearing a letter from Father Willems. He did not yet know the contents but just receiving a letter from his mentor was enough to make grin from ear to ear. He rose and hugged Father Asante warmly for the first time. He peeled open the flap of the envelope and read the contents with dilated eyes, covered with a thin film of tears.

Dear Brother Yao,

I have not kept to my promise. It is true. To confess I held back when I wrote to find out about your ordination and was told about everything that had happened. However, I have always had you in my mind and I have always prayed for you.

Many years have definitely passed. But I felt urged to write and see how things are going.

And I was exceedingly happy about the turn of events. Life is not made of a bed of roses without thorns. Trust me, it is a long time since I took a shot of champagne since I returned to Holland. But that day when I heard the good news I toasted to your good health.

Yao, how about coming to spend a month with me in Holland for a change? Please just confirm it and I'll make the necessary arrangements with the Dutch Embassy and send you the return air ticket.

Yours in Christ

Rev. Father Willems.

Yao shouted, 'Glory be to God' and made the sign of the cross several times as he told Father Asante about the invitation. He could not believe what was happening to him after all the tragedies he had suffered. This time it was Father Asante who embraced him tightly, laid his hand over his head and prayed for him.

When Father Asante left, Yao closed the door to his office and sat down quietly, contemplating about his life so far, and the unbelievable turn of events—the exoneration, the award and now this invitation. He gave up trying to make sense of it all. Sighing he said, 'God you are God and you do what you like. I am the clay, you are the potter. As my Lord said, let your will be done. Do with me what you will and grant me the grace to bear. Amen.'

A sense of peace settled over him and he thanked God quietly in his heart.

For the first time in his life, Yao began to take note

of airplanes as they passed over his house. He looked at them until they vanished. He wondered if he would really be going to

Holland for a month's holiday. Maybe he needed it, to literally resuscitate himself.

He was beginning to recognise that patience was an outstanding virtue. He looked for an encyclopaedia and read about Europe, especially Holland. At church the next Sunday, his prayer of thanksgiving to God was with heartfelt gratitude and a sense of beginning to appreciate God's unfathomable ways.

———— **34** ————

Things moved very fast thereafter. He came to Accra to stay with Celine's family who helped him with all the necessary preparations. The Dutch Embassy in Accra had no difficulty with Yao's application for visa, supported by the invitation from Father Willems.

The flight was scheduled for 10pm. He was travelling by Air France. On the day of the flight the Nkrumahs made it a family trip to the airport to the delight of the children. They arrived in time for the 8 o'clock pre-flight check-in. He quickly hugged the children and Celine, said goodbye and got down at the drop-off zone. Mr. Nkrumah got out and brought out his luggage. He waved them saying, 'See you soon.'

He had his first experience of the flurry of activities at the airport. He took in the scenes with quiet amusement and interest as passengers moved in and out of the building, some pushing large trolleys containing their luggage, others holding simple hand luggage. Taxis, private cars and diplomatic cars pulled up at the glass doors letting out their passengers or picking up new arrivals. Once in a while, an announcement came over the public address system of the next arrival or departure of an airplane or the names of people wanted at Customs or Immigration.

Yao showed his passport to the security man at the glass door who directed him to the Air France counter where his luggage was taken, scanned, tagged and put on a conveyor belt with other luggage and disappeared inside. He was left with his hand bag and he was directed to make his way up a flight of stairs to the second floor of the airport building. He found out it was immigration and customs where he had to fill in forms concerning his journey. He was searched and passed through the body scanner and then shown a waiting area with a row of seats. There were other passengers already there, some were chatting. A lady soon came to stand before a door ahead of them and announced that passengers going to Holland should come forward. Yao again showed his passport and ticket and was given a boarding pass. He and his fellow passengers proceeded down another flight of stairs into a long air-conditioned bus which took them to an Airbus labelled A 300 which they boarded. The air-conditioning in the plane breathed a tolerable chilled air. When the passengers had settled down an announcement came over the speakers welcoming them aboard and giving information as to the pilot who was flying the plane, seatbelts should be fastened till the plane was airborne and the expected time of arrival at their destination. Then a smartly dressed, confident, air-hostess appeared and started giving them safety instructions as to what to do in case of emergency. Yao missed a heartbeat as the plane made the first move forward. It moved slowly onto the runway. It taxied to a point far away from the main airport building then turned slowly into the next runway and prepared to take off. It moved slowly and quickly gathered speed and rose into the air. Yao felt a tremor down his spine as the plane changed speed. He looked through the window and saw the top of the airport building and then the whole of Accra below them. Except for some spots of orange and blue lights, the whole of Accra was clothed in darkness. The plane went higher still. It now floated over a sea of white cotton clouds. Yao sighed, closed his eyes and prayed. He felt a certain relief, as if the burdens of this world that he had been carrying had been lifted off him momentarily. He wished the plane could rather carry him to heaven instead of another world.

——— 35 ———

Holland was indeed an experience he would remember for years. After arrival procedures he came out to the arrival hall of the large Schiphol airport to find a very tall gentleman delightfully waving a card with his name on it. Yao went towards him and said, 'I'm Yao, thanks for meeting me.' They shook hands and the man said, 'I'm Dan. Welcome to Holland. Let me take your luggage.' Yao said, 'Thank you,' and followed him to his vehicle at the car park. The driver's head almost touched the roof of the black Urvan bus on which they were travelling and he had pushed the driver's seat back to give him enough leg room. If there was one thing Yao quickly noticed in the few minutes since he touched down, it was that the Dutch were quite tall. Dan whistled pleasantly to the soft music he was playing but he drove with such frightening speed as if he had an appointment with death. Yao's heart was in his mouth, but he managed to focus his attention on the smooth road. Once in a while he could not avoid admiring the old storey buildings, beautiful vegetation and colourful flowers lining both sides of the road and the numerous dykes holding the water. In no time they were at Gouden Weiken Hotel at Scheveningen, a beach resort in the capital, Den Hague where he was to lodge. It was a long building with many rooms and must have seen better days since there were not many guests that night when he arrived. Although they got to the hotel about 10 pm the weather was cool and clear like an afternoon in Africa. Dan informed him that Father Willems would meet him the following day.

He was shown to his room. He didn't feel hungry. The meal on board the plane was yet to settle down. He needed to stretch out his jet lagged limbs. He changed into night clothes and as soon as he lay down, he slept deeply.

The beautiful buffet breakfast he met when he went down the following morning was nothing he would forget in a hurry. The long flower decorated table had a line-up of all the beverages one could think of, jams and butter of all kinds in small plastic containers, bread and cheese and all kinds of salads and vegetables, meat products and all kinds of fresh fruits. He took some salad, bread and beverage and an apple, only as much as he could eat. He went to the lounge to wait for Father Willems. At mid-morning the latter walked in. He was wearing a tee-shirt over which was a black leather overcoat running half way over his brown trousers. Both men moved and instinctively fell into each other's arms. Father Willems gave Yao a long bear hug and rubbed his thick palm over his shoulder. He pulled away and scrutinised Yao who also sized up Father Willems. The latter had grown very frail and had a more pronounced stoop. His head was covered with matted white hair. He was unshaven and a stubble of white beard covered his face. Large veins crisscrossed his hands and the flesh on his hands stuck to his bones.

'Yao my boy, you are now a man.'

'Yes Father, your son has grown.'

'We should thank God for everything.'

'Certainly.'

Father Willems looked around. 'I think we can sit at the far end of the lounge.'

They sat down and Father Willems made a sign of the cross across the face of Yao and said a short prayer and repeated the sign of the cross across when he had finished.

Father Willems welcomed Yao and the two played catch-up— Yao and the rest of his seminary life, the problem with his ordination and how he had to leave Keta for Adafienu and what he had been doing currently at Adafienu. He also talked about his mother, who had rejoined him.

'By the way, I forgot to ask whether you are married, now that you are not in the priesthood.'

'Father Willems, I can assure you that I'll never marry, ever. I am satisfied with my life as a bachelor. Not because of Catherine. No. I just want to live as if I am still keeping the Catholic priest's vow of being a bachelor.'

A faint smile broke on the face of Father Willems. 'Never say never, my boy,' he said.

Father Willems also talked a lot about his return to Holland and what he had been doing. He told Yao he would be inviting him to see the other pensioners with whom he had been spending the rest of his life, and show him his residence warning him in advance that it was a small place, attached to a Catholic church which had closed down for lack of congregation. He gave Yao a travelling pass to use to travel by train, bus or tram to any part of Holland for the period of his stay. He lamented about how the Christian population was dwindling in Holland and said that there would be the need for a reverse flow of evangelists from Africa— where the church was vibrant and growing— to Europe where it was in danger of dying. The discussions continued late into the afternoon and in between they had lunch at the hotel. Later in the day, Father Willems took Yao to the beach at Schreveningen. There was a long promenade along the beach facing the calm sea. There were rows of beautiful chain hotels with revellers having the best time of their lives. Other revellers were seated at the beach in make-shift open air wooden structures. Chefs in white aprons busied themselves preparing barbecue whose sweet aroma filled the air. Sound systems blasted from giant speakers. In the midst of this festive ambience, knots of Christians courageously sang and distributed Christian pamphlets. That was very heartwarming in this no-God intoxicating atmosphere.

The two men walked silently across the length and breadth of the beach and picked a tram to get back. Father Willems saw Yao to the entrance of the hotel and left, promising to pick him up the following day. True to his words Father Willems came to fetch Yao around noon and first took Yao to where he used to spend the day with the other pensioners. Some were more advanced in age and had to be helped to their seat or anytime they wanted to get up from a wrought iron bench provided in front of the cathedral. Pigeons were pecking at food crumbs on the hard pavement. Father Willems introduced him but attempts at conversation were unprofitable as some of the voices were hardly audible. From there Father Willems took him on a tour of the cathedral whose doors were barricaded in places. To the back of it was an adjoining small room where Father Willems was staying. Yao's heart sank. It was a very small room with just enough space for a bed, a small place to cook and then a washroom housing a bath and toilet bowl. The heater was not working effectively and Yao could feel a biting cold. It was a far cry from where Father Willems lived in Keta. He was consumed by sorrow and wondered why Father Willems would opt to return to Holland.

Father Willems told Yao that the ticket he had bought for him would enable him visit places of interest in Holland by bus, train or tram. He explained that most Dutch speak English and so he would not have any difficulty travelling round Holland.

So for the rest of his days in Holland, Yao travelled widely visiting places like Utrecht to observe the flower fair, then to Amsterdam to have a boat trip on the canal running through the town and then to Rotterdam with its big port and large cargo ships. He also visited the International Court of Justice, the seat of government, and then the Queen's Palace. He subsequently visited the entrancing stores around as well as the African market. He made a lot of notes of interesting ideas of what he saw and experienced. He took a lot of pictures. He had enough materials to teach his pupils about happenings on the other side of the world. These pleasant events notwithstanding, Yao was eager to get back to Ghana, to rejoin his mother Pauline and see to the running of his school. The trip was useful and quite educational but he loved his country and wished to return to it as quickly as possible. He had another two days and that was enough for him to see other places of interest; a special cinema called the planetarium to have a view of the galaxy, then a football stadium in the neighbourhood to watch a thrilling game between some youngsters.

He got some souvenirs and presents for people back at home, especially Celine's children, Nana and Aunt Amega. He and Father Willems had an emotional farewell, promising to write to each other often. Dan came to take him to the airport. As his plane soared into the air he heaved a sigh of relief — another chapter in his life had closed.

—————36—————

M r. Nkrumah met Yao at the airport and he spent two days with the Nkrumahs before returning to Adafienu to a quiet welcome. After a few days Yao went to Dzelukope to greet his kinsmen and see how his mother was faring. Pauline who showed no curiosity for the absence of his son, was looking a bit more cheerful.

Yao gave a brief account of his trip and answered all his relatives' questions. Yes, it was true he was well received by Father Willems. He conveyed Father Willems' well wishes to them. He told them how Father Willems did his best to make him happy but he felt something was missing in the whole Dutch atmosphere, the love of God.

There was a serious matter waiting for his attention upon his arrival. Catherine had sent a delegation to Joseph Johannes. She wanted a meeting to unload herself of the big burden that had plagued her for years. She needed to remove the burden.

Joseph discussed the matter with his grandson who

was not in the least enthused. But Grandpa insisted and despite himself Yao finally had to agree to a meeting.

So it was that early one morning, Yao had to go again to Keta. And Catherine was there with her parents, some uncles and surprisingly Father Asante, very conspicuous in his white cassock. After the exchange of greetings, Joseph invited Kofi Nutifafa, Catherine's father to take the floor. Nutifafa was brief and to the point, 'Catherine my daughter has carried a heavy burden for years, close to a decade. But the time has come when she feels she must ask for forgiveness. The Bible says that there is rejoicing in the presence of the angels of God over one sinner who repents. And again it is said, an ailment of the heart is only felt by the one afflicted. In this case it is both my daughter and Yao, I believe. With the permission of all of you gathered, I would ask Catherine to do what she wants to do by her own volition.'

Catherine went meekly over to Yao and knelt down. 'Please forgive me, for the pain I have
    caused you, for ruining your desire to be a priest.'
    Father Asante asked her, 'What do you mean?'

With tears running like rivulets all over her face Catherine said, 'I started pursuing Yao before he left for the seminary. No matter how hard I tried he refused to have an affair with me. I even wrote to him at the seminary and visited him at Cape Coast...'

'You did what?' her mother shouted.

Catherine continued, 'When I tried all this and he wouldn't give in I decided to destroy him.'

There was a collective shocked intake of breath from all gathered. She continued, 'I started dropping hints of him being my boyfriend. Then I sent a letter to the seminary telling them that Yao is a hypocrite who had impregnated me.'

Amara burst out, 'How wicked can you be?'

Then she turned on her mother, 'And you, Dzidzor would not let us know where she was so the truth could be established.'

Her father said, 'Please forgive us, we did not know our daughter was lying to us…'

Amara could not hold herself, 'Some parents you are.'

Catherine continued sobbing, 'In fact, God has been punishing me. My conscience has been tormenting me all these years till I had no more peace. Please Yao forgive me.'

All eyes were now on Yao and Catherine. Yao looked on listlessly. His tongue was glued to the roof of his mouth.

'Yao what do you have for us?' Father Asante asked.

'Well, let my grandfather speak. Whatever he says, I will accept.'

'No, Yao, you have to speak yourself, it must come from you, the afflicted.'

'I have come to terms with my present situation …' he broke off, his voice choked with emotion. Everybody kept quiet, leaving him to his tortured emotions.

Amara was sobbing softly.

Yao's mind trailed off… his name had been bastardised. His truth had been buried in a cloak of untruths or better still woven into a noose tied around his neck, his only luck being that the noose had not been pulled to snap his neck. Finally, the truth had come out. The good news held captive had finally broken free of its shackles. It was too late though. He had never had an affair with Catherine much less impregnated her. It had been a painful episode. The medicine mostly prescribed by means of advice was forgiveness. He wished the medicine called forgiveness was bottled for anyone in his situation to drink. Indeed, any thought of Catherine was a pain that stared him in the face, but to hold it so much against Catherine would also mean that his emotions had not been impacted by his Christian values. What did the Lord's Prayer say? 'Forgive us our trespasses as we forgive those who trespass against us…' He decided to forgive and prayed for grace to lessen the pain.

A sudden spasm of emotion ran through his being. Before he realised, he burst out crying. He got up and left the room. Father Asante followed him and caught him by the arm. Yao fell into his arms, his chest heaving. After a minute, he disengaged himself from his embrace and left the house. Father Asante followed him.

'As the proverb says, you cannot allow dust to enter somebody's eyes and expect that person not to cry,' Amara said bitterly.

'We are only begging,' Davi Dzidzor said.

'Hmm, what has happened has happened. We cannot change the past. As Christians we cannot fathom God's ways. We accept the apology of Catherine,' Joseph said on behalf of the Johannes family.

With tears still rolling down her cheeks, Amara started a song and the others joined in.

'Now thank we all our God.
With hearts and hands and voices
Who wondrous things has done
In whom the world rejoices
Who from our mother's arms
Has blessed us on our way
With countless gifts of love,
And still is ours today.

Father Asante fell in step beside Yao who was heading towards the beach. They walked in silence. The crying of Yao had changed into whimpering. It was a moment of healing.

Printed in the United States
By Bookmasters